Three

Piper Anderson Legacy Mystery

Danielle Stewart

Copyright

Three Seconds To Rush copyright 2016 by Danielle
Stewart

An original work of Danielle Stewart

ISBN-13: 978-1537637174

ISBN-10: 1537637177

Synopsis

Tara Shiloh knows she's not a drug addict. She's positive she's a good mother and hard worker. So why is she in an alley with a needle in her arm? Waking up in the hospital without her son is terrifying. Being told she can't have him back nearly crushes her. With her memory spotty and the circumstances incriminating, Tara must fight to learn the truth and wrestle with the idea that maybe her son is better off without her.

Reid Holliston defends guilty people for a living and it's slowly killing him. He's certain there is no such thing as a truly blameless client anymore. When his phone rings with a voice from his childhood his jaded views make him certain Tara is just one more criminal claiming innocence. But even his skepticism isn't enough to keep him away.

Best friends from a lifetime ago, the two must find a way to trust each other again in spite of how the years apart have changed them. Can a promise made in childhood be enough to save them both?

Chapter One

Tara's nose filled with pungent fumes reminiscent of her short lived job as a housekeeper in a run-down motel. The place had always been so dingy regardless of how much bleach she used on the rings in the tub or the amount of muscle she put into ridding the grubby walls of marks. Nothing ever really came clean. But the clientele who frequented the facility didn't notice. They weren't on vacation. They were all there to escape, to hide. At the end of every shift Tara would smell like the cleaning aisle of the supermarket and feel like she hardly accomplished anything.

But Tara wasn't at the motel. She hadn't worked that job in over two years. So where was the smell coming from? If her eyes could open she'd be able to figure it out. No matter how she ordered her lids to rise, they would not comply. Other senses began to return, however. Incessant beeping and the hum of people clamoring around her suddenly flooded in. Then hands on her body were the next sensation, followed immediately by stinging. Immense pain tugged and shredded her skin, as though she was being yanked in every direction, about to burst apart.

1

Tara heard a far-off cry, a shriek that petrified her as never before. It wasn't until she felt her vocal chords strain that she realized the scream was her own.

"Calm down," she heard a woman order as her shoulders were pressed back violently and pinned. "We can't help you if you fight."

Open, she demanded of her eyes. *Open so I can make sense of this.* Finally, her eyes complied, letting the bright halogen lights overhead bleed in. There were faces above her. *Strangers.*

"What's happening?" she stuttered out, trying to lift her arms but realizing they were restrained. Her legs flailed until someone grabbed her by the ankles and slammed them down.

"We will sedate you if you don't cooperate," the same nasally and stern voice explained.

"What's happening?" Tara cried out in terror.

"You're in Haultin General Hospital. You're being treated for an overdose." This voice was new. A man with a foreign accent and a slightly softer tone. She focused her eyes on his face and slowly it became clearer. He was a slump-shouldered Indian man with a pockmarked face and large gold-rimmed glasses. His smile was yellow, and his eyes were black and circled in darkness. But there was something comforting about the way he was looking down over her.

"An overdose?" she asked, attempting to move her hands again, forgetting the restraints.

"Stop fighting," the angry woman demanded impatiently. "I can't draw her blood like this." She snapped and huffed, her dramatic noises sounding like a pissed off one-man-band.

2

The doctor's face hovered gently over Tara's. "Can you stay calm for me?" he asked, touching her shoulder firmly. She nodded her head and pinched her eyes closed. Tara wasn't fighting the restraints. She was fighting for reality. If this was a nightmare, she was totally engaged—like no dream she'd ever had before.

A flash of a face suddenly crossed her mind. She saw pudgy overstuffed cheeks that butted up to a round freckled nose. Two almond shaped brown eyes flecked with gold and damp with tears appeared next. Finally, the wispy curls fell across a forehead and it made Tara cry out. "Wylie," she bellowed as she began flailing her arms and legs again. "My son. Where is my son?"

"She's going to pull out her IV," the nurse protested.

"Sedate her," the kinder doctor ordered, sounding apologetic and disappointed.

She didn't hear anything else over her own screaming, as darkness crept in and folded over her body, but she knew the world was slipping away. She tried to fight it as the last few words of the nurse crept in.

"She finally asked about her son. I was wondering if she even cared about what happened to him."

Chapter Two

Tara startled awake to someone scraping a metal chair across the linoleum floor to her bed. She quickly realized her hands were still strapped down, but her senses seemed to have returned. She was fully aware that the dingy yellow walls and beeping equipment meant she was in the hospital.

"Was I in an accident?" she asked with a hoarse and tired voice.

"Tara, my name is detective Nelson Monroe. I'm here to read you your rights and tell you about your arraignment date." The man's crisply starched white shirt never wrinkled as he sat down next to her hospital bed. His heavy gold badge dangled from a chain around his thick, leathery, tan neck. The deep set wrinkles around his eyes could use some of that starch from his shirt, Tara thought as she looked him over.

"Charges?" she asked, shimmying herself to a sitting position and taking inventory of all the wires and lines hooked to her. "I don't understand what's going on."

"Memory loss can be common after an overdose. You are lucky the officer on scene had Narcan. More and more of us are carrying it now that heroin has become prevalent." Detective Nelson was speaking with so little expression that Tara considered searching around for a hidden camera. Surely this was some kind of joke.

"I'm not suffering from memory loss," Tara countered through an exasperated laugh. "I'm suffering from some kind of mistake. I don't do drugs, and I certainly did not overdose."

"Hmm," Detective Nelson hummed as though he'd heard it all before. "You'll be arraigned in the morning. A lawyer can be appointed for you."

"You aren't listening to me," Tara asserted. "Where is my son? I want to see him now." She pulled hard against the restraints again, feeling like a chained dog.

"Your son has been treated for his injuries and released into Child Protective Services. A social worker will be in shortly to speak with you about that." Nelson blinked slowly as he explained this seemingly unimportant information.

"Injuries?" Tara choked, her eyes welling with tears as her mouth dropped open and no more words came.

"Again, the social worker will discuss that with you. I'm here to talk to you about the charges you're facing." He flipped open a small pad and read silently, moving his lips like a child just learning the skill. When he finally caught himself up he addressed her again. "Because of the Good Samaritan and overdose laws you won't be prosecuted for the drug-related charges. But child endangerment is a felony charge because of the degree of risk to the child."

"Where is Wylie?" Tara begged, banging her head back on the pillow over and over again. This was not reality. It couldn't be.

"As I stated he has been treated and released from the hospital and is now in the care of Child Protective Services. The social worker will have more information for you. I'd be far more concerned with the felony charges. I've spoken with your doctors and they believe you will be released in the morning. An officer will escort you to the courthouse. As for a lawyer, do you have one?"

"Should I try to get my own lawyer?" she asked in a barely recognizable husky voice. Her eyes were still stinging from an endless stream of salty tears.

Detective Nelson seemed like he'd been woken from a dream, finally seeing her face and realizing she was more than just a number on his sheet. "If you can afford one," he said empathetically. "There are plenty of good court-appointed lawyers, and there are some I wouldn't let defend my dog. Is this your first time in the system?"

"Yes," she replied indignantly. "I've never been in any trouble before. This is all a big misunderstanding. A terrible nightmare or something. No one believes me. I just need someone to believe me." Her emotional words cracked and faltered as she reached her cuffed hands up toward his arm. And with that, his humanity reabsorbed into his tired body and was gone. She'd played the one card everyone played. She claimed innocence.

"You can get a phone call if you have a lawyer to contact," he uttered flatly as he stood and moved back a few steps. "I'll bring you a phone."

"I don't know his number. I need to look it up."

"Someone will be in shortly to find that number then." There was no goodbye or good luck. He faded out the door of the small hospital room and closed it tightly behind him. The locking noise reminded her how trapped she was.

Someone will listen to me. Someone will finally believe me. This can't go on forever.

An hour passed before anyone came to get her. All her thoughts, every ticking second was dedicated to her son. Part of her felt that if she forgot to miss him, to be desperate for him even for a second, she'd lose him. As if by sheer will of her mind she could stay connected to him until this was all sorted out.

"Do you need to make a phone call?" an old crooked woman asked, as she let her heavy eyelids rise and fall slowly, looking like she could fall asleep standing up. Her glassy grey eyes were rimmed with outdated blue mascara and her yellowed crooked teeth all came to a point.

"I do," she said, sitting up as straight as possible as though her elementary school teacher asked her a question. Maybe the better she behaved the faster all this would go. "There's a lawyer, his name is Reid Holliston. He's based here in Boston. I don't know too much more about him."

The woman didn't speak as she flipped open her laptop and began to hit the keys harder than seemed necessary. Her long red nails punched a number into the cell phone and passed it toward Tara. It took some maneuvering to move her head down close enough to the hand still tied to the bed. As the phone began to ring she suddenly felt like a fool.

"Morris, Morris, Freeler, and Banks," a chipper singsong voice said then paused, waiting for her to speak.

"I'm looking for Reid, I mean Mr. Holliston," Tara forced out. "I'm an old friend of his."

"Oh-kay," the woman on the other end of the phone said slowly and drawn out as though she were dealing with a complete idiot. "Your name?"

"Tara Shiloh," she replied, sending up a silent prayer that her name would still mean something to him. "It's important that I talk with him right away."

"He may be in a meeting; please hold." Before Tara could tell the woman that this was an emergency the line was beeping, indicating she was on hold.

"Hello," a man's voice said tentatively. She tried to convince herself she could recognize it, but the last time she'd talked to Reid was ten years ago.

"Reid," Tara said, swallowing back the emotion, "I'm so sorry to bother you. I need some help."

"Tara?" Reid asked, and the uncertainty in his voice made her worry that she'd overestimated his memories of her. They'd lost touch so long ago it might have been foolish to think this call would be received well.

"I know it's been a long time. We were just kids, but I was hoping you could help me. I need a lawyer. I saw on social media a while back that you worked in the city with this firm."

"Um," he breathed heavily, "I'm actually a defense attorney. I handle criminal charges and felonies. I can recommend a good family lawyer if you need something like that. Is it a divorce?"

"No," she murmured embarrassed to be watched so closely by the woman who'd handed her the phone. "I actually need a defense attorney. I'm not exactly sure what's going on. I woke up in a hospital, and a detective was here telling me I was under arrest and reading me my rights. I need someone who knows me to come help." She could hear how frantic her voice was, but she had no power to stop it.

"I'm not sure that I can help you," he replied stiffly. "My caseload is pretty full. Like I said, I can refer you to someone who I'm sure can help you sort this out. Hang on."

"No," she pleaded, crying now. "My son. They've taken my son from me, and I don't understand what's happening. He's three years old. His name is Wylie, and he must be scared out of his mind right now. He has to be wondering where I am. Please, if you can remember just for a minute how close we were, how much we meant to each other back, maybe that would help. Just remember."

She could hear him breathing, but he seemed at a loss for words. The pause was painfully long before he decided to speak again. "Where are you?" he asked reluctantly.

"I'm at Haultin General Hospital. They are going to release me in the morning and transport me to my arraignment."

"What are the charges?" he asked, still void of any type of emotion about what she'd told him.

"Felony child endangerment," she whispered, as though the quietness would make the words smaller than they were or the situation less daunting.

"Felony?" he asked, sounding shocked. "What exactly happened?"

"I honestly have no idea," she gasped out. She could feel the familiar flutter in her chest that told her she was getting too worked up for her heart to handle. The machines clipped to her body seemed to agree as they began to chirp louder. "I was grocery shopping with my son. The next thing I knew I woke up in the hospital. They told me it was an overdose, but I don't do drugs. You know that."

"The last time I saw you, you were fourteen. I can't corroborate what you've been doing for the last ten years." His voice was as unfriendly as the last two people she'd encountered. "If they are charging you with a felony that means they believe great bodily harm or death was a probable outcome of your behavior. What drug were you using?" He whispered something to someone, indicating she barely had his full attention.

"I wasn't using any drug," she boomed. "I was grocery shopping. I was buying cereal and chicken nuggets. You have to believe me. No one believes me." The familiar wave of anxiety flooded her again.

"Okay," he replied, and for the first time she heard an ounce of reassurance in his voice. "I'll come to the arraignment in the morning and give you my best legal advice. But if this goes to trial, I won't be able to represent you. Lucky for you the state is so backlogged that, as long as you get bail, you'll be walking free for close to a year while you wait to go to trial. More likely you'll end up with a decent plea deal as long as the judge is reasonable."

"My son," she rasped. "When can I have my son?"

"I'll look over the case in the morning before the arraignment. I can't say much else unless you can shed more light on what happened. You aren't giving me much to go on."

"I can't," she apologized. "I didn't do this, and I don't know what happened. There isn't more I can tell you because I don't know myself."

"Right," he sighed in the same tone as Detective Nelson. Apparently pleading innocence was not a very unique stance to take when charged with a felony. She must not be the first person to cry or beg for someone to listen. "I understand. I'll check the court docket and be there."

She waited, hoping to hear him say it would all be all right. To hang tight and not worry. But he said nothing else.

"Bye," she breathed out as the phone disconnected, and she felt the thin thread tying her to someone had just been yanked away. She was alone again even in the presence of these strangers. Whatever reassurance she'd hoped Reid would give her hadn't happened. He wasn't warm and compassionate; he wasn't at all like she'd remembered him.

Long press-on nails were in her face, demanding the cell phone back. "Any other calls?" she asked impatiently as she moved toward the door.

"No," Tara admitted, knowing there wasn't anyone in her life that could help her now. She'd been alone for almost two years. Completely alone. It was only she and Wylie now.

"The social worker is waiting. I'll send her in," the woman said between snaps of her gum.

"Good," Tara replied firmly, a wave of hopefulness filling her. This person could find Wylie. She'd have answers. At least it was a start.

"Tara," a soft voice asked accompanied by a little tap on the door frame. "My name is Emily Corraza. I'm a social worker for the state. May I speak with you please?"

"Yes," Tara implored desperately. "Yes, please. I'm wondering where my son is. Do you know?"

"I do," she replied with a tiny smile. Emily was slender, not a curve on her body could be seen through her flowery blouse and black pants. Her honey-blonde hair hung in a childish braid over her left shoulder. "He's with a foster family right now. I actually dropped him off

11

myself. He was cleared by the doctors and should be fine." Pursing her lips, she had a pained look of apology on her face.

"What happened?" Tara begged. "Was he hurt?"

"He suffered some hypothermia," she explained, crinkling her chin sadly. "He's all right now. A very happy, healthy little guy. I want to talk about some options you have. Can we do that?" Her voice was so melodic and calm Tara nearly forgot how dire the situation was. There was a glow of empathy around Emily that lulled Tara away for a moment.

"What happened?" Tara asked, not bothering to wipe away her tears. She didn't care how wild her hair looked. She was being judged and scolded for things she hadn't done. Let them stare, as long as someone fixed this and fast. "I don't understand how any of this happened."

"I understand this can be very confusing," Emily reassured her, raising a hand to quiet her gently. "You don't have to discuss anything that happened last night with me. That's not why I'm here."

"But I don't know what happened last night. Can you tell me anything?"

Emily sat in the chair by Tara's bed and pursed her lips again, thinking it over. The freckles splattered across her nose and cheeks added to her cherub demeanor. "As far as I know from the police reports and witness statements, Wylie was discovered in a shopping cart in the parking lot of the grocery store. He had no coat on, and it's not known how long he was there before he was discovered by some Good Samaritans. The police were called, and they checked your car's registration for information. About the same time, you were discovered in a nearby alley suffering from a heroin overdose.

Luckily the officer on scene was carrying Narcan. He was able to revive you. I don't know much besides that. Wylie was brought here and checked out. Like I said, he's been medically cleared and released."

"I don't do heroin," Tara insisted, through more tears. "I didn't leave my child in a shopping cart alone in the middle of winter with no coat on. I would never do that. You have to believe me."

"Okay," she said, reaching over and patting Tara's leg. "We don't have to deal with any of that right now. I want to talk to you about Wylie. Do you have any family who would be fit and willing to care for Wylie?"

"I can take care of Wylie," she argued, filling suddenly with rage. "I am fit to take care of my child. I'm going to go to court tomorrow and tell them this is a mistake; they have this all wrong. Then I can have my child back."

"That still leaves tonight," Emily challenged in a non-threatening way. "Is there anyone in your life who we could have Wylie sent to, just while you sort this out? Your parents? His paternal grandparents? A sibling of yours?"

"My parents live on a commune in California. I haven't spoken to them in eight years. I'm an only child."

"Paternal grandparents?" Emily asked again.

"Yes," Tara reluctantly admitted. "Millicent and Todd Olden. They live in Boston. I haven't spoken with them since TJ died."

"Is TJ Wylie's father?"

Tara nodded, unable to conjure up more words.

"I'm very sorry to hear that. How did he die?"

"Heroin," Tara ground out. "But that was his issue. Not mine. I have never used. I didn't even know he was using for a long time."

"Let's not get off topic here. You said the Oldens live here. Do you think they'd be open to caring for Wylie while you deal with the charges against you?"

"I'm sure," Tara nodded with a sarcastic huff. "They haven't seen him in over a year. I was taking him for visits for a little while after TJ died, but it just didn't work out. I'm sure they'd be happy to know they can have him while I'm stuck in here."

"We can have them evaluated to see if their home would make a good temporary solution for Wylie. We'd like to keep him with blood relatives if at all possible." Emily made some notes in a file and looked up for more information.

"They already foster," Tara shared hesitantly. "I'm sure the state would find them very fit for Wylie. I'm the one who didn't think they should have contact with him."

"Why's that?" Emily asked, her face filled with concern. "Was there some kind of falling out?"

"TJ never got along with them. He told me it was impossible to be a part of their lives unless you did everything their way. They treated TJ terribly when he needed them the most. They cut him out of their lives and tossed him aside because he embarrassed them and, in their eyes, tarnished their good name with his addiction. They are heavily involved in their church, and TJ's habit didn't fit into that. I decided anyone who would be so cold didn't deserve to be around my son. TJ didn't want them in Wylie's life, and while I tried for a while to make it work, it just didn't.

14

"I see," Emily cooed earnestly, "but under the circumstances, and in my experience, it sounds as though they still might be the best temporary solution for Wylie. Even with the misunderstandings in your past, they sound like they could care for Wylie in the interim. Do you agree?"

"It's better than complete strangers, I guess. If you're telling me I can't be with him, I can't take him home tonight, then I'll agree to him going to the Oldens' house."

"Good," Emily said, as though Tara had just answered a multiple choice question correctly. The corners of her thin lips perked up and her eyes beamed. Clearly Tara was making this easier on Emily than she was used to. "I'll start making the calls. Here's my card," she said, handing over a pink business card swirled with flowers. "You can call me if you have any questions. I'll ask that you don't reach out directly to the Oldens or attempt to see Wylie until we have more clarity on the situation."

"What does that mean?" Tara asked, feeling like everyone knew something she didn't. The night had been filled with language and processes she'd never known. "I'm going to go to court and this will be figured out tomorrow."

"That's criminal court," Emily explained gently. "Many times charges of felony child endangerment can play out in civil or family court too. It's not listed in the penal code, but being charged can impact your parental rights. It's important you understand that. The state will be involved in Wylie's well-being now, and that might be regardless of the outcome tomorrow."

"It's a mistake," Tara insisted again. "This entire thing. I know the more I say it the less people seem to believe me, but I'm telling you I don't do drugs."

"There was a needle in your arm," Emily said, finally sounding frustrated with her. "But that doesn't mean you won't ever be fit to see your child again. It's a process. One you can help shape. You can get well. You can be the mother Wyle deserves. It takes work—"

"No," Tara shouted, feeling completely out of options now. No one was listening. "You aren't understanding me. I don't need rehab. I don't need help. I need my son. We were fine. Just the two of us. I want that back."

Emily jumped back but quickly righted herself, maybe reassured by the restraints still holding Tara down. "Anger is a common reaction. Also the detox process can be very overwhelming. You aren't alone. I hear you have a lawyer. That's a great place to start. Focus on the criminal charges and take some comfort that Wylie will be with family."

Tara's nostrils flared as she bit back the words she wanted to say. They'd only fall on deaf ears. She'd look like a neurotic fool if she let loose the fury inside of her. "How will I know when he's made it to the Oldens?"

"If you give me your lawyer's information I can communicate through their office when you don't have access to a phone."

"Like if I'm in prison," Tara half laughed and cried. "This is insane."

"It'll work out." Emily attempted to assure her, but it was unconvincing. "Just focus on you."

"I'm a mother," Tara growled. "I haven't focused on me since the day my son was born. I haven't put myself first. I've skipped meals, I've ignored being sick, and I've given up everything for Wylie. I'm a mother."

Emily's eyes glassed over for a beat but she blinked her stubby lashes quickly until the tears vanished. "I'll be in touch."

Chapter Three

Reid stared at the line of trees blowing by him as his car sped down the winding road. He wasn't suicidal. That was for other people. Sick people. He just occasionally thought about hooking his steering wheel and ramming his car into the woods. Everyone felt that way occasionally. Right?

The sports radio station changed to static the way it always did on this patch of road. Everyone always told him he should live where he worked. Why? He hated his job, and driving into the woodsy silence and leaving Boston behind was the only thing that kept him going some days. Even if it meant he had to get up an hour and a half early. Even if he had to keep his car stocked with protein bars for the nights he didn't have the energy to talk long enough to order dinner.

He'd determined what he wanted to do for a living when he was sixteen years old. Mitch Disson's father had come to his school for career day and had spoken so passionately about law and justice that Reid knew if he didn't become a lawyer he'd regret it for the rest of his life. It meant giving up basketball and basically murdering his social life, but he was determined. Reid had an addictive personality, but luckily it had been only for success, education, and money so far. The side effects weren't all that different than someone addicted to drugs.

He was antisocial, losing most of his friends and family somewhere along the way. He'd been too busy, too focused to see them all moving farther away from him. He would lose weight all at once because he'd forget that food kept him alive. And when people started to ask if he was sick, he'd force himself to put the pounds back on.

He had accepted a position with Morris, Morris, Freeler, and Banks two years ago. The firm had a legacy in Boston. Three of the partners had been sharks in their day, but it wasn't their day anymore. Morris Senior had dementia, yet his named stayed on the door and his signature on the bottom of plenty of documents. The cover-up of his medical condition was one for the record books. Morris Junior, normally going by the name Teddy, tended to spend the majority of his day chasing after women half his age and dealing with the fallout. Freeler and Banks were good enough guys, old as dirt and fairly straight-laced. But they were tired, rarely making it to court anymore. That left Reid to carry the brunt of the cases. He had some paralegals and staff at his disposal, but he'd been one of those men angrily accused of never delegating. Busy suited him. When your mind raced about a case it took up space. And that space couldn't be used up by your own memories.

This morning, however, was nothing but memories. That was what happened when a person you haven't seen in ten years came calling. It was like a plug in a tub yanked up and, no matter how hard you try, you get sucked back to the darkness.

Tara had been the skinniest little nobody girl when they met at the park. She was seven and he was nine. They were both latchkey kids, though for very different reasons. His mother and father worked in the city and commuted to their very important jobs. Her parents were hippies or drunks or something, and they just never seemed to be around. The park ran programs where college kids coordinated games and fun things to do for the neighborhood children. At nine, Reid thought that was pretty cool. It was different in the early nineties. There weren't tons of video games or indoor activities. The expectation was: if it wasn't raining you stayed outside.

Tara had been quietly playing cards with the college girl in charge that day when Reid walked up. Her tiny smile was missing half its pearly whites with two big adult teeth that seemed out of place. He had to hold back his laugh at the sight of it. But he did. Because he'd known what it was like to be laughed at.

Reid had been chubby at five but was straight-up husky by that summer. His cheeks were always round and as red as watermelon. Wearing a shirt in the pool was a must and hiding out from the other kids was a survival tactic. But he could tell the first time he set eyes on Tara, she'd never call him a name. She wouldn't shove him or pinch his fat or laugh when he tried to jog. She was the kind of girl who'd flash a sweet gap-toothed smile and make you forget the world was shit for a second. And it worked. Their friendship worked for years. Until he'd failed her. Until he let her down in a way that haunted him in his quietest moments. And now here she was again, begging him for help, and he'd probably fail her again.

Chapter Four

The wood table was so glossy Tara caught the outline of her reflection in the thick lacquer. Her hair was wispy and wild, fighting hard against the elastic band she used to try to wrangle it. Not washing her face last night to get rid of the smeared mascara made her look even worse. But none of it mattered. All she wanted to do was run her finger across the little crevice in her son's chin and smell the sweet scent of his bubble bath.

"Your lawyer is on his way up," the bald-headed bailiff said as he peeked in the room then moved back into the hallway.

It had been so long since she'd seen Reid. She wondered if his curly brown hair would still be shaggy. He'd transformed so much in the seven years they'd known each other; she tried to imagine how the ten years since they'd seen each other had changed him.

There was a summer, a couple years after they met, where his doughy body had climbed upward, sucking in the fat and turning it to height and muscle. His skin cleared and his smile straightened from braces. Over that summer Reid morphed into something completely different. She was sure after all this time she'd hardly recognize him.

But she was wrong. His amber eyes were the first thing she homed in on when he entered the room. His short haircut and well-tailored suit made him look like a stranger, but his eyes, the dark lashes rimming them, and the tiny scar that cut through his eyebrow, were all the same.

"Reid," she said in a gasp of relief. "Thank you so much for coming." She stood to hug him but jolted back as the chains around her wrist held her firmly to the table.

"Are these really necessary?" Reid asked so accusingly that it sent the bailiff snapping into action, yanking at the keys on his belt.

"You're right," he agreed, fumbling with the lock for a minute. "I think if she tries anything we can take her," he joked, but neither of them laughed. He backed out of the room in awkward silence and closed the door.

"Thanks for that," she murmured as she rubbed at her wrists. "I know I'm a mess. I've been up all night."

"I've had a chance to review the charge." Reid launched right into business and the coolness in his voice made her aching heart squeeze even tighter. "Judge Mastlison has been assigned to your arraignment today. That's not terrible. She's very pro rehabilitation rather than incarceration for drugs, however she's less lenient when children are at risk."

"Reid," Tara said sternly, "I didn't do this. I don't need you to help me with the case. I need you to get them to understand this is a mistake. I thought you'd know how. I thought they'd listen to you."

"I've read the report," Reid challenged, an exhausted look in his eye. "They have sufficient evidence to bring this to trial. You don't want that."

"I know I don't. All I want is my son."

"He's been placed with your in-laws. I received word this morning. They seem receptive to caring for him. You

22

will be luckier than most if you keep him out of the system. I'm going to reach out to the prosecutor this morning, but my gut tells me they'll pitch a plea. You plead guilty and in return you'll be remanded to some mandatory drug treatment. Because of the severity of the felony charges, I'd expect at least ninety days. I'd imagine they'd offer one to two years of probation. You're lucky this is your first documented offense."

"It's not my first *documented* offense, it's not my offense at all. I'm telling you I have no idea what happened. I don't do drugs. This is a mistake. You know me."

"I don't," he countered, a bite in his voice, as he banged one hand down on the table, not hard but enough to draw her eyes to his arm. His shiny gold watch gleamed under the halogen lights in the small conference room. Tara knew instantly the divide between them could be summed up by the differences in what they wore on their wrists. Normally, before the hospital had cut it off of her, there was a tiny beaded bracelet she and Wylie had made together. Nothing close to the gold he wore.

Reid drew in a long breath and rubbed quickly at his temple. "I knew you when we were kids. That doesn't mean I know what you do today, just like you don't know what I do today. However, after reading the charges against you, if you don't take this plea you will go to trial, and odds are you will go to jail for anywhere between two and ten years. If you're seeking my legal opinion, I'm giving you advice."

"What happens to my son if I plead guilty?" The tears were coming too fast to catch so she let them meet at her chin and then fall away. This wasn't the kind of emotion she could dam up and wrangle. At its core was

23

sheer dread, the idea that she would never hold her child again.

"I don't deal much with family or civil cases," Reid continued. "But once you are convicted of felony child endangerment, it's not probable your child will be placed back in your care in the near future. Now perhaps after you finish treatment and stay on the straight and narrow for a time, you can likely begin some visitation and possibly get on the road to reunification."

She balled her hands into fists and banged them against the table, far louder than he had. "Are you out of your mind? Is everyone crazy here but me? I am not going to admit to something I didn't do and lose my son. I'm pleading not guilty because I'M. NOT. GUILTY. I thought you'd help me."

Reid pulled a file out of his briefcase and sighed deeply. "Read this," he said, tossing the open report down in front of her. She rolled her eyes, feeling completely ignored, but complied. In the document she saw words that shattered her heart. The description of her son found in the freezing air, abandoned and too cold to even cry. His lips were reportedly rimmed in blue. His shivers so violent they looked like convulsions. Her eyes could take no more. The visions of her suffering child proved too much to bear.

Farther down the report was the documentation of her own condition. She'd been found stuffed below a dumpster, presumed dead by the original caller who had not been identified. The officer who first arrived at the scene recounted uncovering her lifeless body with a needle still hanging in her skin. She quickly folded the file and slid it back to Reid, who seemed to refuse to sit across from her. That would be far too much commitment, too much intimacy, and he didn't seem willing.

"That's all the jury will see," he said, more gently now. "I've been defending people long enough to know it's not always about the truth; it's about what they can prove, and from where I sit the case against you is strong. Massachusetts is inundated with heroin and overdose deaths. It's an epidemic. When people read that statement, when they hear the eye witnesses who found your son, sitting alone in a shopping cart behind your car with no coat on in below freezing temps while you were down the street getting high and nearly dying, it won't matter what else is said. That's all they'll hear."

Tara clutched the desk with both her hands, trying to get the world to stop spinning. Trying to will time to stop until things made sense again. "If I plead not guilty and I win the trial, will I get Wylie back?"

"That will be played out in civil or family court. But if you are completely acquitted your odds of retaining your parental rights are better. However, the current state of the system means it could be eight to twelve months before you go to trial. And going into the family court system before you have a resolution to your criminal case could be tricky. If you are determined to go to trial, I would encourage you to allow your in-laws to have temporary custody of your son. Don't rock the boat, and there's a chance if they're supportive you won't need to address a more permanent solution until after you go to trial, but again, I have to reiterate that in my opinion you should consider the plea that will likely be offered to you. Either way you're not likely to have your son back in the short term. It's important you understand that."

She lost her breath as though someone had just closed their hands around her neck. "Help me, Reid," she pleaded again, hopping to her feet. "You know me. You know that I wouldn't do this. Remember when I was nine and Mary Sullivan wanted to go around and collect money from people for that magazine thing? Remember that."

"I remember," Reid admitted but had an air of irrelevance. She waited for the spark to light in his eye, the corners of his mouth to turn up a little. But neither happened.

"I wouldn't do it. I said it was wrong to take that money. They were tricking people. I cried my eyes out and no one talked to me for two days. But I was right. That's who I am. I don't hurt people. If you can imagine, for just one second, what it would mean if this was all a mistake, all a terrible nightmare, wouldn't you help me?"

"The needle was in your arm," Reid reiterated, unwilling to suspend reality long enough to allow himself to agree with her. She knew that was what was required—he'd have to ignore all the evidence and just believe her. A tall order for an analytical man like Reid.

"Just for one second, Reid, believe me." She stared so fiercely into his eyes, refusing to blink. "How would you help me if you knew I hadn't really done this? If you knew without a doubt I was innocent, wouldn't you help me?"

He shook his head as though it took all his energy not to raise his voice. "Innocent isn't a term I use frequently in my line of work. But if you're asking me how I'd form a defense, I would scrutinize the police investigation. Sometimes the simplest case can be overturned because of a mistake or oversight. I'd dig into the cops that found you, the witnesses, and anyone else involved and try to undermine their character or credibility. I'd stall. I'd coach you on how to be a sympathetic woman. I'd fight to make sure the jury was made up of people who might fall for that. If I was going to defend you I'd use every tactic I had to get you acquitted."

She narrowed her eyes and tipped her head to the side as though he'd just admitted to a crime himself. "That's not what I asked," Tara whispered. "I don't want you to undermine someone else in order to prove my innocence. I don't want tactics and tricks."

"That's what a defense is." He chuckled. "That's what I've been doing every day of my career."

"But I'm innocent," she argued, her brows knitting together.

"Every single client I've ever defended from white collar crimes to manslaughter has said the exact same thing. I make sure of it actually. I only want to be told the minimum. I don't want a confession. And they all know better than to give me one. They say they are innocent, or framed, or crazy and then they actually start to believe it, no matter how much evidence is piled up against them." His arms were waving animatedly, and she imagined what he looked like in court, pleading someone's case.

"Are you good at it?" she asked, raking her eyes over anything on him that seemed familiar, any small characteristic that would remind her of the sweet boy she knew years ago.

"At my job?" he asked indignantly. "Yes. I'm good at it. But what does that mean really? I'm good at getting guilty people their freedom?"

27

"You hate what you do." Everything else melted away for just a moment. She wasn't worried about herself or Wylie; there was Reid and the sinking feeling that came from watching his face crumple in pain. He'd done so much for her when they were young, but she always knew when something was wrong.

"We're not the same people anymore, Tara. You don't know me, and I can't help you." She took the slightest bit of comfort that at least it pained him to turn her down.

"Then go," she whispered, pointing at the door with her tear-soaked chin. "Leaving right now won't change my plea. I won't admit to something I didn't do."

He made a move for the door but stopped suddenly. "Why me?" he asked, turning his broad back, like a wall he'd built himself. "Why did you call me? Was it just because you had no one else to call?"

She thought on it for a moment. "It's not like I had a list of lawyers in my cell phone," she admitted. "But I would have called you even if you were a plumber or a taxi driver."

"Why?" he asked, turning enough so she could see his profile, which was painted with curiosity.

"Because I knew you'd come."

Chapter Five

"Good morning," Judge Mastlison offered, and it seemed too bright and cheery for the situation, in Reid's opinion. Everyone in the small courtroom replied obediently.

"I see some familiar faces this morning. Mr. Holliston, it's been a bit since I've seen you in my courtroom." She looked over her thick glasses that sat low on her nose. Gray curls streaked with a few strands of black sprang up all around her head. "And Miss Umbers, I see you're back in the rotation for the DA's office."

"Yes, Your Honor," Chelsea Umbers answered politely. Her suit was gray and boxy, altogether ill-fitting. "It's a pleasure to be back in your court." Her slicked back and pinned up hair never moved as she nodded nervously.

What only a few people in the room knew was that Chelsea Umbers had been accosted by a defendant after a guilty verdict was read in his case. The college athlete convicted of raping and beating a girl from his dorm had hired one of the most expensive defense attorneys in the state. The defense they made was weak and based mostly on the fact that the man's baseball career was too promising for him to make such a stupid mistake. *Mistake*, Chelsea Umbers had scoffed as she annihilated

29

the defense. The only mistake the defendant had made was leaving so much evidence behind.

With a few quick jumps the freshly convicted athlete had broken across the courtroom and made it to Chelsea before any of the officers could reach him. It was just two punches but they were enough to knock her out cold and fracture her cheek and eye socket. Reid knew, however, the incident had damaged far more than that. The chatter in their circle was that it had destroyed her confidence, rattled her to the core, and was in jeopardy of ending her very promising career. But apparently she'd rallied because Chelsea had been assigned this case.

"Since we're all familiar with each other," the judge continued, "let's keep this moving along efficiently. Mr. Holliston, you and your defendant have been given a list of the charges, I assume." She folded her hands, coolly looking up with an air of impatience.

"We have," Reid replied dutifully.

"And the district attorney has provided you with the details of a plea deal in return for your client pleading guilty?" the judge continued, glancing at the documents in front of her.

He heard a tiny noise escape Tara, and he drew in a breath, begging her silently not to interrupt or disrupt the court. "We have," he replied again, but this time blowing out an exasperated breath.

"And how does your client plead?"

"Not guilty, Your Honor," Reid said, straightening his back some, knowing this was just the beginning. He could feel Chelsea's coal black eyes on him from the prosecutor's table and the judge riffled through a few more pages as she began to speak, an air of concern in her voice.

"Your client is aware the district attorney is offering a ninety-day drug treatment plan and three years' probation, deferring all jail time as long as the terms of both are met?"

"She is aware." Reid kept his gaze level.

"And your client understands that upon conviction, these charges require a sentencing of one to ten years in prison?"

"She is aware of that as well," Reid said, and then silence closed in around them all as the judge slid her glasses closer to her eyes and read more from the papers in front of her.

"Your Honor," Chelsea finally interrupted, "the defendant was in the hospital until this morning. The district attorney's office would be open to a recess that would allow counsel to discuss the terms of the plea deal."

"That's not necessary," Reid asserted, straightening his blue striped tie. "My client is fully aware of the information provided and is unwavering in her plea. More time will not change her mind."

"What am I missing here?" the judge asked, finally dropping all the documents down and pulling her glasses off completely, waving them as she spoke.

"My client asserts that she is innocent and would like the opportunity to prove that during a trial. She's been informed of consequences if she is convicted."

"Well that didn't answer anything," the judge huffed. "How about you, Miss Umbers? Can you shed any light on the situation?"

"I, uh," Chelsea hesitated looking over at Reid as though he were a jerk. "I've read through the police reports, the witness statements, as well as the hospital report on the child's condition. The District Attorney's office feels the degree of risk, which could have resulted in great bodily harm or death, met the threshold for felony child endangerment. I can't account for why the defendant is opting to go to trial."

"Mr. Holliston," the judge sighed, "obviously it is your client's decision on how to plea, and if she has been fully informed of the options, we will move on and the plea will be entered into the court records. However," she drawled out, now staring at Tara, "I would like to hear it directly from her."

"My client," Reid started but stopped abruptly as the judge raised her hand. He looked down at Tara and gave her a tiny nod.

"Your Honor," Tara started but her shaky voice betrayed her. Clearing her throat, she forced the words out. "I didn't endanger my son, and I didn't abandon him. I would never do that. I don't know what happened or how I even ended up in this situation, but I want to find out as much as anyone else because I want my son back. So I won't plead guilty."

The judge nodded but didn't look impressed or pleased. Chelsea's voice rang across the court layered with annoyance. "I hope that counsel has informed his client that being high and not remembering is not a defense that will gain acquittal. There is ample precedence for that."

"I'm not claiming I don't remember because I was high," Tara cut back, but the gavel was hitting the desk, the loud banging eating up her words.

"Please inform your client not to address the court unless she's been asked to."

"Yes, Your Honor," Reid apologized.

"I'll be honest," the judge cut back, "I'd like to understand why your defendant believes acquittal is possible, considering the information in these documents."

"I'm not sure the exact information you are referring to," Reid lied.

"The needle in her arm," Chelsea huffed. "The baby in the hospital."

"Easy, Miss Umber," the judge cautioned.

"There was no investigation," Reid asserted, stuffing both his hands confidently in his pocket. "My client woke in the hospital and informed anyone who would listen that she was not a drug user. She was clear with the officer who came to read her her rights and gave the same story with the social worker. Yet as far as I know there was no investigation. Where is the security footage from the grocery store? Her record is clean; she's never had a drug violation or history of drug treatment."

"She had heroin in her system," Chelsea argued as though this was all nonsense. "Are we trying this case right now, because I was under the impression this was an arraignment."

"Please don't make me regret welcoming you back so warmly," the judge said, though there was still some kindness in her voice. "I've heard enough. If the defendant has made her plea, let's discuss bond and trial date."

Before Reid could interject, Chelsea stepped out from behind the large desk and launched into her point. "Considering the charges—"

Reid interrupted with a firm voice. "My client is not a flight risk. She has no passport, a car that doesn't look like it could make it out of the city limits, and no contacts with anyone outside of the state."

"Everyone can be a flight risk," Chelsea replied flatly.

"She wants her son back, and she's determined to follow the correct channels to make sure that happens," Reid argued.

"The district attorney's office would, at a minimum, require she not have care, custody, or control of any child under the age of seventeen." Chelsea had a bite at the end of her words. She was back in the game.

"The court agrees," Judge Mastlison said with the strike of her gavel. "One thousand dollar bond, and let's set a date for this trial."

"I'd like to petition for an expedited trial date," Reid said, knowing again how this would be perceived and wishing this day would just end. He couldn't wait to be shifting the gears in his car as he sped toward his quiet house.

"Why?" Chelsea asked rather unprofessionally, but he couldn't really blame her. "You just determined that you intend to build a case where today there is none. Now you want less time to do it? With all due respect, Your Honor," she turned her attention back to the judge as she spoke. "I'm concerned this could be grounds for an appeal after conviction citing ineffective assistance of counsel."

"It's a little early to be calling me incompetent," Reid fired back, not sparing a glance in Chelsea's direction. This was turning a little more personal than he'd planned, but it happened sometimes. It was actually nice to hear Chelsea with a little fire in her voice again. She hadn't deserved what happened to her.

The gavel slammed down hard again. "All right, back to your corners. Mr. Holliston, you should know the earliest I see to set the trial date is sixty days from now. I'll grant it, but I don't want to see you in here asking for an extension. You can't have it both ways."

"Understood," Reid assured her. "The sooner the better." It was a good thing he wasn't under oath right now because the Bible he'd have to lay his hand on would burst into flames.

"Anything else?" the judge asked, her gavel hovering ominously over the desk. Both Reid and Chelsea replied that there would be nothing more today.

"You'll both be notified about motion and plea deadlines as well as expert witness and evidence disclosures. Court adjourned."

Chapter Six

"You didn't need to pay my bail," Tara edged out nervously, rocking back and forth on her heels as she tightened her arms and tried to stay warm.

"Did you want to stay in jail?" Reid asked flatly, and she shook her head no. "Did you have anyone else willing to pay?" For the second time she shook her head no. "Then I had to pay your bail. Now here's some money for cab fare back to your apartment. They had your car impounded so I'll make calls tomorrow to get it out."

"What do we do next?" she asked, feeling as small as she ever had in her life. Since becoming a mother Tara had learned to fight. She fought the nagging loneliness that came with her isolated life. She fought the exhaustion from nurturing and loving someone more than herself. But at that moment she had no fight left. If Reid smelled the way he had when they were children, that bubble gum and licorice type of sweet, she'd fall into his arms right now. But he didn't. He was all musk and aftershave. He was altogether different. A stranger.

"Nothing tonight. But come tomorrow we'll need some resources. You and I will talk, then we'll argue and get aggravated and you'll beg me to stop asking you questions but I won't. I need to know every detail of your life because at this very moment that prosecutor is out turning over every rock and looking for your secrets."

"I have none," she protested.

"No more tonight, Tara. I can't. I've heard all I can for one night. We'll start again tomorrow. Just go home."

"It'll be empty," she sniffled, bringing a sleeve of her too thin coat up to wipe her freezing nose. They were standing on the stairs of the courthouse and the wind was whipping in their direction. She was desperate to get something from him, some kind of comfort or strength.

"This should cover the cab." He slipped a few bills into her hand and walked away. It was too late in the evening, the sun dipping down too low behind the tall buildings for her to be able to see his face as he crossed the street. It was all shadows and emptiness. *He was all shadows and emptiness.*

After watching him disappear toward a parking garage she stared at the money in her hand. It was more than enough to grab a cab home, and she was sure he knew that. It would get her dinner and a tank of gas once she had her car back, too. She watched a few yellow cabs roll by and considered raising her hand to flag them down. But she didn't. Tara wasn't going home. There would be a thousand little things that would remind her of Wylie. And that ache was so deep she thought it might split her in half if she faced it.

Her feet began shuffling forward before she formulated an exact destination. But there was a pull, a siren's song of need inside of her, and she'd follow it. She had to.

Chapter Seven

"Get in the car," a sharp voice yelled in Reid's direction as he walked across the parking garage.

"Christ, Kay you scared the shit out of me. What do you want?" Reid didn't make a move to get into Katelin Star's red Camaro. He hadn't been in it since he broke things off with her nearly six months ago.

"Get in, we need to talk." She leaned across the passenger seat and flung the door open.

"About what?" he asked, finally sinking down into the seat with a huff. "I've had a long shitty day, and I'd like to be in my car on my way home."

"Chelsea called me just now," Kay explained as she shifted the car into gear and took off out of the parking garage.

"Where are we going?"

"Chelsea called and told me about the case. What the hell are you doing in there? Are you having a quarter life crisis or something? Did you hit your head?"

"Chelsea doesn't have a clue what she's talking about," Reid attempted, but he knew an astute lawyer like Kay and an articulate woman like Chelsea would have had plenty of time to hash out the details of what was going on and probably have a hundred theories of why.

"I won't say anything to her about it. She wasn't asking me to dig anything up. I honestly think she was a little worried for you or your client. I know for a fact that your plate is full with your firm. They dump everything on you. I know you are sick of all these rich bastards hiring you to defend them for crimes they commit. But have you actually cracked?"

"I haven't," he replied, unsure if that was the truth or not. "I have a client who refused a plea deal and is asserting her innocence. I'm going to defend her. It happens all the time."

"Not in these types of cases," Kay argued, and Reid knew he was too tired and emotionally drained to win.

"From what I gather she has no money to pay you, you have no time to try the case, and there is no case to be made. I know you like to punish yourself but this is a true lose-lose situation."

"How do you figure?" Reid asked, tossing his hands up in defeat as Kay circled around the city aimlessly.

"If you lose the case she's likely to go to prison for at least five years. If you win it, and she's guilty, you'll free a mother who left her child to die in a shopping cart while she did drugs. After being acquitted she'd be on a pretty expedited path to get her child back. So tell me that one little thing you're hiding, because it's written all over your face."

"I know her," he coughed out in annoyance.

"You dated?" Kay asked, then corrected, "You're dating now?"

"No," Reid huffed. "We knew each other as kids. I haven't seen her in almost a decade."

"Yet you feel obligated to represent her?"

"I owe her," he spat out but then immediately remembered he had no intention of sharing that information with anyone. It was their secret. His burden.

39

"We were very good friends for many years until she moved away. She's in a jam, and I want to help her."

"Convincing her to take the plea deal was helping her."

"I tried."

"You have more time. Try again. You can still motion to change her plea. I know Chelsea would be open to it."

"She won't," he said, shaking his head. "She says she's innocent. She's convinced of it."

"Are you convinced?" Kay asked in a very small voice as she pulled the car over, knocking the rim against the curb as she did.

"I don't need to believe her to defend her. You know that about my job. It's basically the only rule."

"It's the part you hate the most. It's the part that had you staring at the ceiling when I'd wake up in the middle of the night and look at you. That one little rule is crushing you."

"I'm not crushed," he scoffed with a shrug. "I'm right here and I'm fine."

"You could leave the firm and come over to the DA's office. It's a cut in pay at first but you can work your way up."

"This is the same argument we had once a week for the majority of our relationship. Do you really want to have it again?"

"No," she admitted, "but there are a lot of things I wish didn't have to happen again. There's this dark place you go, this island in yourself that you'd row your boat toward and then throw the oars away. It scared me when you headed that way. You deserve happiness." A familiar defeated droop fell over Kay's face, and he remembered instantly why they were not together.

"I really am fine," he lied as he patted her shoulder as formally as possible, considering their history. This post-breakup arguing had twice before turned into a kiss. That turned into another night together. But it had to be done now. For her sake.

"I don't believe you but if I keep you here much longer, I think it turns into a hostage situation," she said through a little forced laugh as she shifted in gear again and sped down the road toward the courthouse. "Just promise me you'll be careful and call if you need me. I don't have to agree with you to help you."

"Thanks, Kay," he said, averting his eyes from her warmth, feeling repelled by her kindness, so polar opposite it pushed him away like the flip side of a magnet. As the world moved by him, like the shutter of a camera clicking over the city, there was a flash of Tara. The pinned up hair, the same outfit she'd had on in court today. There she was, not in the cab he'd told her to catch. Instead walking down the street toward the seedy road leading to the old factory affectionately known as pill palace. "Damn," he murmured before he could stop himself.

"What is it?" Kay asked in that way she always did when he started to falter. It happened more frequently than he liked to admit.

"I forgot I have a meeting in the morning with Fisher about a case we're wrapping up. I overbooked myself," he covered quickly. "Guess I better get my shit together."

"Why start now?" She giggled lightly as they rounded the corner and pulled into the parking garage.

"Don't forget to call me," Kay purred, smiling up at him as he lifted himself from the car and turned his back.

Watching her cherry red car pull away reminded him of the day he'd finally broken things off. He could have married Kay. No, he *should* have married her. She was the kind of woman who fought to make sure he was happy.

Plans were always made for him so he could have some kind of social life. She kept him fed and fit and well rested. Kay cared. She meant it. He'd be happier now if he'd stayed with her. But the same could not be said for Kay, and that was the point. For every improvement she brought to his life, he diminished hers in some way. Not maliciously. Not intentionally. But that didn't change the reality. It took a lot of work to keep a man like Reid happy. Because his natural state was anything but. It was a job. And the only way to save Kay from that burden was to emotionally fire her. Tonight, listening as she laid her help at his feet once again, he knew he'd done the right thing.

The long car ride home was calling his name. Blaring music, an energy drink, and a power bar for dinner. The winding road would be just what he needed right now. Even if he had the urge to chase Tara down and stop her from using his cab fare to buy her next fix. It wouldn't matter. Not right now. She'd have to be clean for the trial. But tonight he could hardly blame her. That was the thing about addicts, they were nothing if not consistent.

Chapter Eight

Twelve years earlier

"*Tara, you are such an idiot.*" *Thomas Dorrady laughed as his beer spilled out of his red Solo cup onto her dress. It was the first time she'd worn it and her prepubescent body wasn't filling it out the right way.* "*What kind of party did you think this was?*"

"*I'm going,*" *she said, trying to push past him but blocked under his grip on her shoulder.* "*Just let me go.*" *Her voice was as small and ineffectual as her fists would have been against Thomas's ruddy pocked face.*

"*You're here now, might as well party.*" *Thomas pushed the red cup into her face, but she slapped it away, sending it flying and landing with a splash to the ground. A fire brewed in his eyes, but it wasn't anger. It was some type of twisted pleasure in her fighting back. As if her acting out would warrant and excuse whatever he wanted to do next.*

"*What the hell? Do you know how hard it was to get that beer? You owe me now. How you going to pay up?*" *His grip was crushing as he backed her to the closest wall of his parent's basement and tipped her head up with his free hand. She focused her eyes away from him, not giving him the satisfaction of her attention. Instead, blinking through the threat of tears, she stared at the*

43

knots in the old wood paneling. Some looked like faces, crying out for help. Others looked like angry monsters.

"Back off, Tommy," Reid's voice demanded as he closed in on them. Relief flooded Tara's body at the sight of him. Their friendship had changed after the summer pulled them both in different directions. She was twelve and Reid was fourteen; it had a way of dividing them like the shifts of tectonic plates. They'd smash together and pull apart. But he still cared for her, and he wasn't going to let some jerk hurt her. She knew that.

"Mind your business, Reid; she spilled my beer." He never took his eyes off Tara, looking at her body in the way most boys did lately. His tongue ran over his lips like Tara was an appetizer.

"I'll spill your brains all over this floor if you don't let her go," Reid threatened, moving in closer, and although Tommy didn't look back at him, she felt his grip start to loosen. The glint in his eyes, the mischievous one that terrified her, melted away.

"Come on, Tara, I'll walk you home." Reid reached his hand out and she took it quickly, sliding out from under Tommy's arm. She saw Tommy open his mouth to protest and his hand came up to grab back at her, but Reid's stiff arm slammed into his chest. "I'm serious, man," Reid said in a low voice. "I'll destroy you right here in front of all your buddies and embarrass the hell out of you in the process."

"Why do you give a shit about this poor little piece of trash? She's a freak."

"If I see you touch her again you won't even hear me coming for you," Reid said. "I'm talking about ever. At school, on the street, wherever, you don't go near her

again," he hissed as they walked up the basement stairs, his hand on her back.

It was impossible for a little girl not to fall in love with a guy like Reid. He was a sweetheart who had been wrapped in the muscle of a newly changing body. He towered over most of the other boys, and his shoulders had started to broaden well before theirs. It meant he was on every sports team, on every girl's list, and yet he didn't seem to take notice of anyone or anything in particular. To her he was still the little fat kid she'd met at the park years ago who couldn't seem to keep his balance or stay out of the bully's way. And maybe that's why he was still loyal to her, because she'd stood by him when no one else cared to.

"You shouldn't have come," Reid scolded as they headed down the street to her house.

"I didn't know it was that kind of party," she argued. "I just thought it was like, you know, a birthday party or something." Her cheeks blazed with embarrassment, knowing now how stupid she sounded.

"I don't know how you're going to make it through this life the way you are," Reid said, his face softening as he glanced at her from the corner of his eyes and crammed his hands into his pockets, slumping his shoulders forward.

"What do you mean?" she asked, feeling even more self-conscious of his assessment. The age gap had never really meant much between them until he began to change. There was a time they were about the same height, and she could hardly picture that now.

"You are too sweet, Tara. That's not a compliment. You have to be stronger than this, smarter. Someone is going to hurt you someday. What did you think Tommy

45

was going to do to you if I hadn't come in? Seriously. I want to know if you know."

She shrugged. "Push me around or something?" She had an idea of what a guy like Tommy would want with her, but she wouldn't know the right thing to say. And she was getting so tired of saying all the wrong things to Reid.

"Guys only want one thing from girls, Tara. You can't put yourself in a position where you're alone with someone like that. Especially if he's drinking. He'll hurt you. You'll understand it someday, but until you do you just have to trust me. Because, like I said, I don't know how you're going to make it if you keep being so sweet."

"I know how," she smiled with half her mouth as she looked at him. "I'll have you." She nudged at his side with her bony elbow, but he didn't laugh.

"You might not always have me," he said, a frightening worry washing over him. From a guy who never seemed to get worked up about anything, this was freaking her out. "You need to learn to take care of yourself. Promise me."

"Where are you going?" she asked, taking a few large steps and diving in front of him so he had to look her in the eye. "You know you can't leave, right? I've got no one else. You know my parents; you know what they do."

"Forget it," Reid said, glancing away. "Just promise me you'll be more careful. Don't trust anyone. You can't."

"Can't I trust you?" she asked, walking again with him, tucking her hands in her pockets too.

"Yeah," he sighed, "you can trust me. You can always trust me. But no one else."

"Okay," she nodded, her short bobbed hair dancing back and forth. "And you can trust me, Reid. You know that, right? I swear it. I know there isn't a ton of stuff I can do for you, but you can trust me."

"I know, kid," he said with a laugh as he patted her head affectionately. "I can trust you."

Chapter Nine

"Thanks for getting my car out," Tara chirped as she lowered herself into the chair across from Reid. "Your office is really nice." It was a large space with windows behind him that looked out over a quiet row of trees. The desk was a rich cherry wood with fancy notches carved into the edges. Warm beige walls were adorned with paintings, but nothing hinted at his personal life. Just some framed degrees and art that looked specifically designed for a professional space.

His eyes were on her, scrutinizing with a hint of anger. "Thanks," he finally edged out, looking more tense than he had during their time together in court.

"Are you all right?" Tara asked, leaning back and folding her arms across her chest self-consciously. She'd taken a shower, brushed her hair out, and put on her only decent outfit. But the look in his eyes was making her feel like a heap of garbage.

"I'm fine; how about you, are you fine? Are you clearheaded enough to have this conversation? I don't need to be wasting my time. I put off two other meetings to have you up here. If you're going to be turning down drug treatment, I hope you have some other plan for yourself. You'll need to be clean for trial. Otherwise there's really no point to this."

"What are you talking about?" Tara laughed but stopped abruptly at the look on his face. "I told you I don't need drug treatment. I don't do drugs."

"Did you take that cab home last night?" The arrogant look on his face made Tara's stomach knot up.

"Are you following me?" she asked indignantly, feeling like if she couldn't get Reid to believe her, twelve strangers would surely never give her the benefit of the doubt.

"I happened to see you," he said bitterly, straightening some papers on his desk. "Listen I would be crazy to assume you'd kick the habit all in one night. All I'm saying is we need a plan to make sure you're clean by trial time. You need to be open to that."

"Pass," she said, nibbling angrily at the side of her mouth.

"What?" Reid twisted his face in frustration. "What are you talking about?"

"Pass; don't you remember?" Tara's mind, which had been pushed to the brink by sleep deprivation, had to wonder if maybe this wasn't Reid. How could he have forgotten their code words and their secrets?

"I . . . uh . . ." He faltered, narrowing his eyes at her. She would have sworn he was a stranger until he ran a hand over his cheek and rested it under his chin. The way he always had when she drove him nuts.

"That's what we used to say." She smiled, wishing he'd remember it as fondly as she did. "If something got too heavy between us, if we couldn't get the other person to see things our way, we'd say pass so we didn't kill each other."

"Tara, this isn't a game." He sighed, leaning back in his chair. "We aren't kids anymore. You could go to jail.

You might miss your son growing up. I need you to do what I ask of you."

"Just pass, Reid. It's not that I won't do what you want, I'm just saying let's move on to something else. There must be other things we could do first. Why argue right out of the gate?"

"Fine," he acquiesced. "We need resources. Expert witnesses and an investigator. The police had you pegged as guilty from the first moment. They didn't look any further into the case. That alone might be enough to create some reasonable doubt in a jury."

"How much does all that stuff cost? I know that your hourly rate must be way above my budget, but I want you to know I'll do what I can to pay you back. Even if it takes me a lifetime." She crossed her finger over her heart, another piece of their own, long-forgotten language.

"Forget that right now. I'll cover the cost of the investigator and call in some favors. There's someone I've known a while. I asked her to join us this morning. It took some persuading, but I think she'll have a good perspective, even if she doesn't take the job."

"Okay," Tara said in a tiny voice, feeling like she was overextending her friendship with Reid. She'd relied heavily on the past relationship between them but now she was sure she was exploiting that part of Reid that could never say no to her. If that was her only path back to Wylie she'd have to get right with it.

"Her name is Willow. She's based in New York, but she owes me a few favors. She's willing to come up for a while and hear you out."

"And she's an investigator?" Tara had wrongly assumed the investigator would be some big-bellied old man, retired from his detective job and looking to freelance. In her mind she'd conjured up an image of an old time Dick Tracy.

"She's more than an investigator. She runs an innocence project that helps people who have been wrongfully convicted. This isn't in her normal protocol considering you haven't been convicted yet."

"Yet?"

"I mean it's earlier than Willow normally jumps on a case, but she was willing to come today. That's a start. She's the best at what she does. I've never seen anyone so driven at what she believes. You want her in your corner, so remember that. She has a family of her own and working with us will be keeping her from them. It's a lot to ask."

"Got it," Tara said, happy that no matter what Willow was like, they had that one common thread; they were both mothers. Surely she'd understand the horror Tara was feeling.

"She's going to ask you things you might not want to answer. Don't get defensive. Hear her out. Nothing she throws at you will be worse than what the prosecutor will be asking." Reid looked at her with an intensity that demanded an answer.

Tara nodded, but like a dammed river finally cresting she asked the questions she knew Reid did not want to answer. "Are you sure there is no way I can see Wylie? Not even for a few minutes? I think if I called the Oldens, even though we haven't gotten along in the past, they'd let me see him. He must be asking for me all the time. I'm his whole world."

"No," Reid asserted. "It's not a good idea right now. Focus on the case." Reid didn't blink. He didn't soften his gaze or mollify his voice.

"That's easy for you to say; you don't have kids. You can't imagine what it's like to not be with him right now. You don't know the agony." She clutched a hand to her heart and the tears began to form again. "I brush his teeth every night and sing this song about *Pearl the white tooth*. I remind him to take potty breaks. This is the longest I've ever gone without him lying in my arms to fall asleep."

"Good," Reid said, looking her over appraisingly. "You need to continue to play that card, be sympathetic." He waved his arm like a director instructing an actress.

"You think this is a card?" Her eyes shot wide open with disbelief. "You think this paralyzing pain of not having my son in my arms is some kind of act? I know every single inch of him, every freckle, every cry. I know him better than I know myself. I love him more than I have ever loved anything, and not being with him right now, imagining he's scared, imagining he's missing me, is the most crushing thing I've ever experienced, and trust me Reid, my life hasn't been easy."

There it was. Finally, a break in his steely expression. He swallowed so hard his Adam's apple jumped. His cheeks changed just slightly, the quick burning red of a firework that fizzled out just as quickly. It was unfortunate the only thing that had rattled him also confirmed Tara's presumption of why he was here helping. Guilt. At the sound of hearing confirmation that her life had been littered with troubles, she knew instantly he felt blame for much of it.

"She'll be good on the stand," a smooth voice said from behind Tara, sending her jumping. In strode a bronze-skinned woman with large eyes and bluntly cut blonde hair. Her clothes were casual, just a gray T-shirt and some well-fitting dark jeans, her black flats looking almost like slippers. Rope bracelets laced around her wrists and an intricately wound metal necklace hung long on her. She was well put together yet intentionally disjointed.

"Willow," Reid announced, standing quickly and pulling her in for a hug. *A hug?* Reid had seemed so stiff, so unfamiliar and cold, but now he was throwing hugs around. Clearly this was more than just a professional favor. "How's the family? Is Josh still working at the clinic?"

"He is," Willow announced with a dramatic roll of her eyes. "He's a glutton for punishment. But he's doing some good, and you know how important that is to him. My husband the martyr." They both laughed and Tara felt small, like she didn't belong.

"I always said he should wear a cape to work. I don't know how he does it. All those treatment programs and sad cases. It has got to be exhausting." Reid shook his head and flashed his familiar friendly smile at Willow. There was a time in their lives that Tara and Reid had their own body language. It was all gone now, saved for other people.

"He must be a superhero to put up with me," she joked as she leaned against the small bookshelf below the window. She didn't opt for the chair next to Tara, probably a tactic to stay noncommittal to the situation.

"I appreciate your making the trek up here. Your opinion on the case means a lot to me." Reid settled back into his chair.

"I'd imagined you'd be interested in more than my opinion; I figured you'd want my services." She cocked one of her brows and challenged him. Then she smiled, letting him off the hook.

"I didn't want to start begging too early," he said with a wry show of his teeth. "You and Josh have been key players in so many of these cases, and I don't know how I'd have gotten through some of them without you. I respect you both a lot and . . ."

"Are we already to the flattery stage?" Willow laughed, waving him off and pushing her bangs off her face. "Let's hear what we're working with, and I'll let you know how I can help. You know Josh and I will do anything we can for you. Now who are we trying to get out of jail?"

"No one's in jail yet," Reid said, his voice sounding cautious.

"I don't hop in before trial," Willow said, tipping her head in annoyance, like she was reminding a child there would be no dessert before dinner. "It's messy and not my area of expertise. But you already know this, yet I'm still here."

"This is Tara," Reid said, gesturing down at her. He gave Willow the run-down of all the information he had so far, and Tara moved her glance nervously between the two of them as he did. Willow had one hell of a poker face. No matter what Reid said she never flinched.

"I know it sounds crazy," Tara finally chimed in, realizing on paper and without perspective, her side of the story was far-fetched and full of holes. "I'm telling the truth. I just need help proving it and—"

Willow cut her off, looking apologetic but unwavering. "I'm sure by now Reid has told you the intricacy of the justice system is not solely balanced on proof or truth."

"Not so eloquently," Tara said, flashing a quick smile at Reid then turning her attention back to Willow. "He's told me I don't stand a chance."

"I started down this path," Willow said, beginning to pace the room, spinning her necklace around her finger, "when my older brother Jedda was arrested for murder. He spent most of his life in prison for that crime until people began to listen, until they began to step in. It inspired my career and changed my life when he was freed. I got my brother back and understood what impact we can all have on the justice system."

"He was wrongfully convicted?" Tara asked with a tiny spark of hope, a sense of *me too.*

"No," Willow said with a shake of her head. "He killed two people who happened to be our parents. But the trial was not adequately handled, and there were enough loopholes to get him free. There were representation issues. It took a lot, but with perseverance he's living a great life right now."

"But he was a murderer?" Tara asked and regretted it immediately when Reid cleared his throat with annoyance. He'd warned her to be respectful, abundantly grateful, and instead she was being accidently insulting.

Willow only laughed. "Technically, yes he was. And that's my point to almost everyone I come into contact with during these situations. If you are looking for black and white, right or wrong, you will most certainly be disappointed. Some killers shouldn't be in prison, and some innocent people get sent there. I work to make sure the law is followed, the person given due process. That's not the same as proving someone innocent."

"But I am innocent," Tara insisted, wide eyes passing back and forth between Willow and Reid, begging for their reassurance. Wasn't it enough to just be right?

"Pass," Reid said with a nearly imperceptibly lift of the corner of his mouth. "There are other things we can do. We don't need to fight on that one."

Tara reluctantly nodded. At least he was remembering what it was like to argue with her. It wasn't ideal, and she wished he would back her wholeheartedly, but moving forward was more important than his true support. "Where do we start?"

"We start where they'll start," Willow announced, finally sitting down next to Tara. A wave of earthy perfume came with her, and it calmed Tara for a moment. She smelled like a mom, soft and clean. "But where they stop, we'll keep going. While the trial itself is far more Reid's department than mine, I can lead the investigation."

"You're ready to sign on?" Reid asked, looking skeptical, like it had been too easy to sway her.

"Normally by the time I get the call it's already too late. It's an uphill battle to free someone. I've been feeling burned out lately, I could use a good fight where we could actually get a jump on things." She crossed her legs and leaned in toward the desk. "Plus, even though you haven't said it yet, I get the feeling Tara isn't some stranger who stumbled across your doorstep yesterday, looking for a lawyer. So if she's important enough to you, you know Josh and I are in."

"Thanks, Willow," Reid said, and Tara took note of the way his eyes could not hold hers. There was a time when emotions, real ones, didn't send him into a panic. "So we know there was little to no actual investigation," he continued, regaining the original thread of the conversation.

"I can't entirely blame them," Willow said, flipping through some papers Reid had handed over. "I mean the dots weren't very hard to connect. The child was found at 9:02 p.m. in the back parking lot of the grocery store. The registration to the car nearby led them to Tara's name, and then Tara was found at 9:27 p.m. about half a mile away. She had her identification on her and the officers were able to piece it together."

"But Tara held true to her story with each person she spoke to. It could have sparked some sort of follow up but it didn't. It's our opportunity to prove some reasonable doubt." It was refreshing to hear him consider the idea that she wasn't some drug addled liar who abandoned her child. "Are you ready to start answering some questions, real answers?" Reid leaned back in his chair and eyed her like a principal with a troubled student. "Anything said in this room will be kept confidential, and we need to know what the prosecutor is going to find out about you."

"I've been answering your questions honestly; you just don't like my answers," Tara argued, louder than she meant to. "But fine. Ask me whatever."

"How long have you been using drugs?" Willow started, seeming unfazed by the tension growing in the room. Her pen hovered over a notebook, waiting for the answer as though she'd just asked Tara to spell her full name or give her date of birth. As if it were nothing at all.

"I don't do drugs." Tara drew in a deep breath, in order to keep from screaming.

"Um," Willow started but then pushed past it. "All right. If that's the stance you're going to take you'll need to know what the prosecutor will do to prove otherwise. Everything has a trail."

"Things that don't exist don't have a trail," Tara countered, tossing her hands up. "I feel like we're wasting time here. I'm not going to just tell you what you want to hear."

"Fine, let's prove it then," Willow said, sounding completely unconvinced. "The prosecutor will look for financial indicators that you have a drug problem."

Tara grabbed a pen and paper and scribbled down some information. "That's my online banking sign in. I have one account. My paycheck from the deli goes in once a week, and the newspaper delivery money goes in every two weeks. The money I get for teaching piano puts gas in my tank. Absolutely every dime goes to an expense you can track. I'm not buying anything that isn't for the survival of Wylie and me. It's all food, utilities, rent. I usually have about eleven dollars left at the end of every month, and that's only if I spend a couple days a week eating only cottage cheese and crackers so that Wylie can have food. I don't have drugs, and I don't have drug money. So what's next?"

Willow looked taken back by the candor, or maybe the desperation, in Tara's voice. But she pushed through nonetheless. "They'll look at associates of yours. Other people in your life that might be addicts."

"I have exactly zero friends. There are a few people at work I chat with from time to time but nothing more than that. People I used to know, before I had Wylie, they aren't in my life anymore. It's him and me. I'm doing everything I can to give him a decent life, and I haven't met many decent people to introduce to him so I don't bother. Check my phone records."

Willow jotted down some notes. "Reid says you don't have any criminal history or drug charges; that will help. But the prosecutor won't back down there."

"What else could she possibly say? I've never been in trouble for drugs, I don't have money for drugs, and I don't hang around people who do them. What else is there?"

Reid rubbed the bridge of his nose as he spoke. "There are other ways to make money that wouldn't go into your bank account. Prostitution is frequently associated with drug use."

"Reid," Tara cried, "I'm not a hooker."

He flinched but didn't let that quiet him. "You asked what else the prosecutor would pursue. There won't be anything that's considered off limits or out of bounds. You should prepare yourself for that. At the end of the day your blood work confirmed you had drugs in your system. They'll flash the photos from the crime scene, they'll show your son freezing in the cold night air alone. And they'll say you probably sold your body for drugs."

"Why won't you help me?" Tara folded over into herself and cried. "Why is this happening?"

"He is helping you," Willow corrected. "He's preparing you for what's going to happen. He's giving you a chance to change your plea. Lying to you and telling you he believes everything is going to be all right might feel good now, but when that cell closes in around you, it won't do you any good."

"Even if you say you don't do drugs, and no record of drug abuse can be found, the prosecutor will claim maybe it was your first time. That doesn't change the situation." Reid moved like a bulldozer over any emotion and barreled toward the facts.

"But," Willow chimed in, "if all of what you just told us checks out it will help create some doubt. It's important. I'll take point on it and get you a report on anything I can find by the end of the week." She was talking to Reid now, cutting Tara out completely as though she were irrelevant.

"How about issues with your son?" Reid asked, flatly. "What is the DA's office going to dig up about you as a parent? What do we need to know?"

"Nothing," she sniped, the insults feeling so raw now. "Everything I do is for him."

"The father," Willow jumped in, both of them completely emotionless in their questioning. "Where is he?"

"He's dead," Tara said as though that should slap them back some. She was a young widow, a single mother, and they were stomping on her relentlessly.

"How long has he been dead and how did he die?" Willow pursued, her face still unaffected.

"An overdose," Tara admitted through gritted teeth. "Heroin. Sixteen months ago." If only they could be convinced her blazing red cheeks were from anger and not guilt.

"Tara," Reid said, jumping to his feet. "Why didn't you tell me this? Did you not think it was relevant that the father of your child died just over a year ago the same way you almost did?"

"TJ didn't do drugs when we met," she protested. "He was hurt at his job, messed up his back, and started on pills. I had no clue it was even a problem until it was too late. I told him rehab or never talk to us again, and he walked out. He left us with nothing, like we never mattered. Do you know how hard I've had to work to keep us fed with a roof over our heads? You can't imagine."

"How do you manage it?" Willow asked, abruptly changing the subject though Tara didn't know why. Maybe she was defusing the tension in the room, or she was one of those people who never read the moment right. "You've got no friends, no support system." She checked the papers again, looking for any indications otherwise. "You didn't graduate high school. Boston isn't a cheap place to live. How are you doing this? Where is Wylie when you go to your job at the deli?"

"I have a sitter for him," she said, running a hand over her aching head. "I work second shift at the deli from three until nine. Wylie and I deliver papers in the morning. It's early but it's a job I can take him along. I teach piano at the high school one morning a week after the paper delivery. When I have a lesson Wylie sleeps. He loves the piano. He sits right in his stroller and goes out like a light."

"The sitter," Reid asked. "You can afford a sitter, rent, a car with insurance. How does the math add up?"

"I don't pay the sitter much. Her name is Cindy. I'm teaching her to play her keyboard, and she can help herself to any food in the house when she's there. She lives in the apartment next door."

Danielle Stewart

"How old is Cindy?" Willow asked reluctantly, not seeming to want to hear the wrong answer.

"Ten," Tara said, but hurried to qualify it. "She's a good girl, very responsible for her age."

"You're leaving your three-year-old son home with a ten-year-old child for over six hours every day?" Reid asked, not even fighting the conclusion in his voice. "These are the types of things the prosecutor will put into play. It goes to your judgment, and the jury will form an instant opinion of who you are as a parent based on that."

"Whoa," Willow said, raising a hand up. "I hear what you're saying, Reid, but dial it down some. Yes, we have to flush these things out and be ready to answer for them when the time comes but we do not need to cast our own opinion. You know better than that."

"It's too late for that," Tara said, blinking off angry tears. "I have a pretty clear idea of what Reid's opinion of me is."

"The good news is," Willow interjected quickly, "we are all clearly dedicated people who can unite behind a common cause. Let's make sure we try to keep the emotion out of it."

Reid nodded like a child who'd been scolded and knew he deserved it. "We do need to be on the same page."

"How long do we have?" Willow asked, again changing the subject. "I can give you a solid week here. Then Josh will need me back home. I'll do the rest of the work remotely and commute here as you need me."

"Sixty days," Reid croaked out, and it wasn't until that moment that Tara realized how big of a problem their timeline must be. Judging by Willow's visceral reaction it was as if he'd just cursed, said the foulest thing anyone had ever heard.

"Oh Reid, why?" Willow asked, dropping her head down. "The docket should be backed up. Did you actually request an earlier date?"

"We're trying to have this settled prior to going to family court and addressing the custody issues." It didn't matter how evenly Reid said it, Willow was still furious.

"I'm going to be blunt here," Willow began, and Tara was getting the impression blunt was her normal speed. "I think your judgment might be compromised. Rushing a case for any reason is a bad idea. You know that."

Tara watched Reid's face, trying to catch the corners of it, searching for him to agree. She was desperate to believe his judgment was intact.

"Noted," he said with a level glare. "We've got time. We can pull something together."

"I'm jumping right in then," Willow said, hopping to her feet. "I'll be at the downtown hotel I stayed at for the last trial. Keep me posted."

It seemed a lot less like Willow was ready to leave and a lot more like she was bailing on the growing tension. Tara couldn't really blame her.

"Thanks again, Willow. And tell Josh I appreciate him living without you for a while. I'm sure he's got his hands full with the kids." Reid softened his tense face again. Something that seemed to happen every time he spoke about Willow and her family.

"I don't know," Willow shrugged with a smile. "He looked pretty excited about it. So did the kids. When Dad's in charge it's all *wear that underwear twice* and *mac and cheese for dinner every night*." She dipped her head and stepped out of the office, leaving behind an awkward silence that made Tara's skin prickle.

"Why can't you believe me?" Tara asked. The words had been running in her mind for so long, repeating on a loop, it was impossible to keep them contained. "If you could only tell people who I am, what you know about me."

"Should we address the elephant in the room?" Reid asked, his nostrils flaring. "I like to leave the past in the past, but I can see you're not willing to do the same. You're confused. It's going to hurt you in the long run, so I'll just address it now."

"I'm not confused," she blurted out, pounding her hand on his desk.

He straightened his back and flattened his tie as he stood. "Just because you lied for me, I'm not going to do the same for you. The situations are different. We were kids. If that's why you called me, because you feel like I owe you, then I can't help you."

Tara stood, angry tears filling her eyes but not spilling over. "I've been hurt in my life before, Reid, hurt in ways you can't imagine. But I expected it. Those people had given me every reason to expect the pain, but you . . ." She choked on the words but forced them out. "Maybe you're right, maybe we're not the same people we were back then, because I don't even recognize you."

Storming out was shortsighted. She knew that. Tara needed Reid. He was the best path back to Wylie. And she really believed that somewhere deep down he was the boy she loved. But right now it seemed buried impossibly deep.

Chapter Ten

Reid had been gone most of the summer. Basketball camp meant a whole new bunch of friends for him and experiences Tara would never be a part of. There was more and more of that happening, and unlike other things Tara had gotten desensitized to in her life, this hurt more not less each time.

"You're back," she sang, jumping up into his arms as he hopped off his bike and dumped it on her grass. "I hate this stupid town when you're gone." They lived in a run-down area west of Boston. Not busy enough to be the city, not quaint enough to be suburbia. The undesirables from downtown wandered in and out often enough for the streets to be dirty and occasionally dangerous, but not hip and busy enough to be fun.

Reid squeezed her tightly, lifted her up, then planted her back to the ground. He felt entirely different. In four weeks he'd grown firmer in the shoulders and biceps. His shaggy hair was cut short and his oily skin was clear and clean. There was something else different about his face, but she couldn't place it. She, on the other hand, was exactly the same. Her flat-as-a-board chest was pathetically unchanged. Tara's height hadn't broken the five-foot mark yet. She was a child, and he was quickly turning into a man. It was like they'd begun together on the starting line, spent some of the race jogging next to each other, but now she was just standing in his dust as he sprinted ahead. It hurt more than she'd ever admit out loud.

"I can't stay long," he said as they sank into the porch swing, and she passed him a soda. "I've got plans."

"I don't," she pouted, pulling her legs up to her chest. "Who do you have plans with?"

"You don't know her." He shrugged, taking a long swig of his drink. She finally figured out what was different about his face. He'd cleaned up his overgrown eyebrows, getting rid of all the stray hairs. It made him look clean and put together. Even better looking if that was possible.

"Her?" she asked, sounding accusatory but quickly changing to a laugh. "A girl? Ooooo."

"Cut it out," he said, shoving her with his shoulder. Not an uncommon move for him but this time it hurt. "Sorry," he said, rubbing it gently and looking horrified that he'd caused her pain. "I didn't mean it. That was too hard."

"I'm fine," she said, rubbing the spot that was sure to turn to a bruise.

"I keep forgetting how little you are." He said it casually as though it wasn't horribly mean to point out how stupidly small she was.

"I'm exactly as little as I've always been. You need to start remembering how big you are. You don't want to crush that new girlfriend."

"She's not my girlfriend," he said, pointing a cautionary finger at her. "You're worse than the guys at camp. I couldn't get a free second with Mary without one of them jumping in and causing a huge scene."

"She was at camp with you? I thought it was just for guys?" It would have been better if she could keep the heat of jealousy out of her voice, but being thirteen meant having almost no poker face.

"Mary's the coach's daughter. She wasn't supposed to hang out with us but we found ways to be around each other. Coach would have killed me if he found out. She lives two towns over, but we're going to take the bus and meet in the middle at the mall."

Tara was desperate for the sentence to continue. For him to just add on: *Want to come?* But he didn't. He just took more swigs off his sweaty and dripping soda can and acted like this wasn't cruel. *"So what have you been doing this summer while I was gone?"*

She shrugged and bit at her lip, angry at him and angry at herself for feeling so stupid. He wasn't going to wake up one morning and be in love with her. That wasn't how things worked in the real world. Being older than she was didn't matter for a long time and then suddenly it did. It would have been easier to just face the truth, but a crush was like gravity. You could pretend they didn't exist but when your ass hit the pavement with a thud and bang, you knew there was no escaping it. No changing it. No outrunning it.

"Come on, you must have done something fun," he encouraged, but she still didn't answer. The tears forming in her eyes gave her away. *"What's the matter?"*

"It's been a crappy summer so far," she breathed out and held her head up to the sky. *"My parents have been a nightmare. I just wish they'd leave. You know? I wish they'd just go and leave me here."*

"Are they fighting again?" Reid asked, shifting to face her.

67

"No," she said in a half laugh half cry. "I wish they were. They're so caught up in this church thing or spiritual enlightenment. I don't even know what it is. Basically they just smoke weed all day and preach. They sound like lunatics now. I liked it better when they hated each other. Now they've combined their crazy behind one cause. This one guy is trying to get them to move to some commune in California. I hope they go. They're never here anymore anyway. I'm alone all the time. They don't buy food or anything."

"Don't say that. If they go you'll have to go too." The fear in Reid's eyes reminded her for a second that he did care deeply for her. Maybe he wasn't going to lean across the swing and kiss her. Maybe he'd never see her that way. But it didn't diminish the fact that he always came through for her.

"I'm not going to live on a commune," she said, wiping at the stray tears. "I'm serious. I have an aunt in New Hampshire. She has this cabin on a lake. I'll go live there. I know she'd let me."

"You can't leave," he said, dismissing the idea with a shake of his head.

"What do you care? You've got Mary." Tara rolled her eyes and made a funny face at him, levity in this dark moment of reality.

"Hey," he said, not taking the bait and allowing her to joke this off. "I don't care who I date or what happens, we're going to be friends for life. Don't you believe that?"

"Yeah," she sniffled, trying to convince him she agreed. It wasn't like she wanted their friendship to be over. But she knew it would end. She didn't believe it would happen all at once. It would take the natural

course of a campfire. Roaring, dwindling, flickering, and dying out. Forgotten.

"I'll cancel my thing with Mary. I'll call her house before she leaves. Can I use your kitchen phone?"

"Don't do that," she insisted. "I'm fine. My parents are out for the rest of the night. Some sleepover retreat thing. There's a monster marathon on tonight. I'll be fine."

"You hate those movies. They scare the hell out of you. I always force you to watch them." He tipped his head to the side and raised a skeptical brow in her direction.

"Things change," she shrugged as she hopped up off the porch swing. "Enjoy your date," she smirked, pulling open the screen door and heading into the black hole that was her house. The smell of stale marijuana smoke and rotting dishes instantly clouded around her.

"Grab your bike," he said, smooshing his face against the screen door. "We'll watch it at my place. My mom will order pizza . . . but no pineapple. That's so gross."

"Go on your date," she protested, laughing as he pushed his nose up against the screen impersonating a pig.

"Get your bike," he said and then oinked loudly.

"What are you going to tell Mary?" she asked, with a sigh.

"I'll tell her the truth. My best friend needed me." He pulled the screen door open and waited for her to make a move toward him. When she hesitated he stepped inside, grabbed her by the arm, and pulled her back to the porch. "Some things change, Tara, but not everything. We're not going to change."

Chapter Eleven

Reid felt like a piece of garbage. Bringing up the moment of their past that had pulled them apart was something that should have been handled tactfully. With kid gloves and a calming voice. He knew better than to bring it up in the heat of the moment the way he had. That seemed to be the theme since Tara had plowed her way back into his life. Reid knew better than to take on a client in Tara's situation. He knew better than to expedite the trial date. He knew better than to table and push away all his other clients for someone who couldn't afford a tank of gas let alone an hour of his legal fees. *But this was Tara.*

Over the years he'd let his mind water down his memories, smoothing them out like a rock rolling in waves, tide after tide. It took off all the edges, all the rough spots that mattered and left a sanitized version of what their friendship had been. The more years that passed between the last time he'd seen her, the easier it was to call her just a friend he had when he was young. Just a kid from his neighborhood. Just some girl he used to know.

Today when she was a couple feet away from him, and her brows shot up the way they used to when they were kids arguing over something dumb, the lies he told himself grew hollow. Tara had been an important part of him and perhaps the most loyal person he'd ever met.

But what did that really change about the here and now? There was still a child who had been left in the cold. There was still a needle in her arm. She'd brought these things upon herself, and it wasn't for him to rescue her. It was different when they were kids. He saw the glow of innocence around her, the bubble that he never wanted to see popped. Like a knight in battle he took a silent oath to try to keep her exactly how she was. Little. Safe. Happy. But a long time ago he failed, and it was a bell he couldn't unring.

His phone rang and the noise reverberated off the walls of his sparsely decorated apartment. Reid had searched for months to find a rental that offered the perfect combination of solitude and ease. The landlord lived in Florida and as long as the rent check arrived Reid never had to hear from the guy. He'd moved in a minimal amount of furniture because he was a cause and effect kind of guy. Don't want to cook? Don't buy pans. Don't want to have company? Don't have food. Or drinks. Or anything remotely welcoming.

"Hey, Willow," he said flatly, answering his phone reluctantly. He would have preferred to send it to voice mail but Willow deserved his attention.

"I know it's late," Willow apologized. "I just wanted a chance to talk with you privately."

"I figured you'd call. Actually I expected you to be knocking on my door. You must be getting lazy in your old age."

"I'm out front."

He peeked out through the wood shutters and laughed. Hanging up the phone he pulled open the door

71

and gave her a defeated little grin. "Are you regretting your choice to help?"

"I never regret trying to help a friend, but maybe you don't need the kind of help you think you need. Are you sure you have a clear head? You obviously have a history with Tara. You don't have to tell me what, but if it's getting in the way of her case then recuse yourself."

"We grew up together. She was a friend," he paused, wracked with guilt, "but we lost touch after she had to leave. I think she was maybe fourteen and I was sixteen."

Willow nodded as though his explanation shed some real light on the situation. "I've been checking into everything she said today. It's early but there is actually a chance she's not an addict. I don't see anything that points to the fact that she is. You know the signs. I didn't see any track marks. I didn't really even see any withdrawal symptoms. She showed up at her jobs every day. She's reliable. That's not what heroin addicts do. They can't hold their lives together as well as she has. We need to start considering other reasons she might have been in that alley."

"You can't seriously be considering her story?" Reid shook his head and rubbed at his tired eyes. "You don't do fairy tales. The reality is she tested positive for drugs, she had a needle in her arm, and she was overdosing."

"I'm not saying she didn't abandon her child and go take drugs. But maybe it was the first time." Willow propped a hand on her hip and demanded he listen.

"A jury isn't going to care all that much in the end. Whether it was her first hit or her hundredth they'll still see it as neglect." He rolled his eyes and knew he was getting dangerously close to pissing her off, not a good idea.

"You know the law better than I do," Willow admitted, though he could tell there was more she had to say. "But I'm a good judge of character and something about Tara has been nagging at me. Josh sees drug addicts every single day. I've been exposed to plenty of them, and Tara does not fit the bill in any sense. Something she said I can't get out of my head. The boy's father died of an overdose of the same drug she was using that night."

"Yeah, I know. The DA will already know that. It'll play awful with the jury. They'll just assume the poor kid had two deadbeat druggies for parents." Reid shrugged as though Willow was wasting his time, but there was a part of him that was dying to hear if she'd come up with some explanation.

"They may think that, unless we prove there is no history of drug use on Tara's part and give them another explanation."

"What else could have happened?"

"I've spent the day tracing her steps and finding out more about her. She wasn't exaggerating about not having any friends. She doesn't call anyone. No text messages. She's alone. Tara goes to work, takes care of her son. That's it. Do you know what that kind of isolation can do to a person?"

Reid knew exactly what total isolation felt like. It was his goal most days. But he still didn't know what Willow was driving at.

"When my oldest was born it changed my life. If I didn't have a huge support system in North Carolina, I wouldn't have made it. I had family flying up, phone calls every day, encouraging letters. I had Josh right there helping me, and we were financially stable. She has none of that. It's all her."

"Are we working on sympathy for the jury?" Reid asked with a sigh. "I'm assuming you have a point."

"One you'd probably never understand. Not until you've been up in the middle of the night with a baby who won't stop crying. Not until you've gone a full day without eating and not even realized it. When a child throws up on the last pair of clean sheets or pours the gallon of milk on the floor, you get it. You know my history, and I've had some hard moments in my life."

"That's an understatement." Reid had heard almost every detail of Willow's childhood and subsequent challenges. Raised by abusive parents who were later killed by her brother, she saw her share of heartache. In later years she got mixed up with a bad boyfriend who caused her more problems. But Willow was like an egg: when dropped in hot water, she'd grown more solid. Whereas some people would fall apart, she seemed to have found her purpose even though it had taken unconventional methods to do so.

"Motherhood has been one of the most rewarding but challenging things I've ever done, and to think of the circumstances under which she's doing it," she paused and shook her head. "Maybe it just got to be too much. Maybe the baby was upset in the store and maybe she used her last dollar to buy food. Maybe it all fell in on her at once. And she knew what heroin could do if you took enough of it. She knew what it did for TJ. It was a way to end it."

It was like he and Willow had been sitting in a dark room and finally the light switch had been flipped on. "Suicide?" he asked, soaking in everything she'd said now that it was in context. "You think maybe she was attempting suicide?"

"It's possible. Think of what that might mean for the case." Willow finally crossed the room and pulled one of the two barstools out from under the kitchen counter and sat.

"I could bring a psychologist in and walk through the stress she was under. A jury would certainly be more sympathetic to an overwhelmed mom looking for a way out rather than a drug addict looking for a fix." The wheels in his head spun as he took the new information into consideration. "What if there is an angle of postpartum? I may even be able to get the charges reduced if I file a petition disclosing the new information."

"I thought there was a chance that it could be reduced from felony child endangerment down to a misdemeanor. I know Tara's goal is a path back to her son. She'll need treatment and monitoring, but this is certainly a more manageable obstacle to overcome than drug addiction. Especially a heroin addiction. Though it still makes me sad for her that she felt that lost."

"Yes," Reid said, slamming a hand down on the kitchen counter animatedly. "It's something anyway. How confident are you that she isn't a habitual user? You've only had one day to look into it."

"I'm going off my gut and what I've seen so far. I still need to talk to her coworkers, the people who live in her building. I'll need a couple more days to vet it out completely. Don't talk to her about it yet. Have her meet with a psychologist. Keep moving forward on the case, and I'll have an answer for you by the middle of the week. But by looking at her, do you really think she's an addict?"

Reid had been asking himself that question every five minutes since he first saw Tara at the courthouse, and his answer was complex. Tara seemed exhausted, nervous, and frantic. But he'd sat next to plenty of users in his life, and she didn't have that kind of twitchy energy he normally associated with a user. She wasn't asking for a fix or worried about where she'd be at any point of the day, not preoccupied with how she'd fill the need. The only thing she was obsessed with was getting her son back.

Reid rubbed at his temple. "Want a drink?" he asked, reaching for a bottle he kept on the counter. He didn't have many glasses but snagged a couple of old mason jars when she nodded.

"You know," she started as she took a long swig of the amber liquid he'd just poured, "I tell my husband all the time all I want is some peace and quiet. My hotel is completely quiet, and I keep thinking about my kids." She took the rest of the drink into her mouth and gestured for him to refill it.

"I'm not one for sleeping either. It's like eating—one of those annoying things we need to do to stay alive. You're welcome to stay and work the case if you want. Maybe you'll have another one of those brilliant epiphanies." He tipped his head back and finished his drink, not wanting Willow to feel bad about swigging hers back so quickly. It was a two-hundred-dollar bottle of Scotch, meant to be savored and sipped but he wouldn't say anything, even as she reached for more. With the amazing work she'd done already, she'd earned it.

76

"I've been over her bank and phone records. In the morning I'm going to check out her medical history. The boy's too."

"Good, I imagine the prosecutor will be scrutinizing that as well, looking for a history of any abuse or neglect."

Willow slid the satchel off her shoulder and pulled out her laptop. "You sure you don't mind the company? I don't want to interrupt anything you had planned."

"I'll cancel the dinner party," he laughed, checking his watch as though the time mattered. "It was a pretty impressive guest list but they'll understand. I was going to make a nice roast." He spun off his stool and headed for the fridge. "Instead I can offer you a ketchup packet, a jar of questionable looking olives, or a protein bar."

"You need help," she groaned, rolling her eyes at him. It was funny. Willow was a mom, a grown woman, but there were still moments Reid could see what kind of kid she'd been. There was an element to her attitude, a fight for power, never let your guard down, that always bled through. Never hesitating to call someone on their shit, or tell them what she thought of them. In Reid's opinion it was one of her finest qualities. "I've known bachelors in my life, but you are like professional grade. I'm going shopping for you tomorrow."

"You've done enough," he said, tossing her a protein bar. "I'm not looking for a mom. I'm a big boy."

"I'll tell you, as a mom, it was hard listening to Tara this morning. She's a strong woman. I hope this works out for her."

"I don't do hope anymore. This job will stomp that nonsense right out of you." He refilled their glasses, forgetting the price tag of the bottle, and realizing this stuff was meant to be consumed. It wasn't all that often he had someone to drink with.

"So, you and Tara, how good of friends were you back in the day? I'd like to have known you then. I feel like you would have been a sweet kid."

"I'm not sure she'd agree. We were best friends, when I wasn't doing something to screw it up."

Chapter Twelve

"Are you drunk?" her squeaky voice asked through the crack in her partially opened bedroom window.

"Buzzed," Reid lied, but the slur gave him away. "Are your parents out? Can I crash on your floor again?" He knew she'd say yes. Tara could never turn him away. With one hand holding him up, he lifted his foot to climb in.

"Why do you keep doing this?" she asked, sounding annoyed but lifting the second floor window open the rest of the way. He'd become a pro at scaling the porch on the side of her house and gaining entry without having to use the front door. "Seriously?" she asked, her hand perched high on her hip as he fell clumsily through her window and to the floor. He stared at her and from his perspective, lying flat on his back, caught a new angle. Something he didn't remember seeing before that moment. There were a few key curves to her body that hadn't been there the last time he looked. Or maybe he just hadn't looked all that close in a while. Tara was wearing only a thin, oversized night shirt and some skimpy shorts she'd recently outgrown. From the floor her legs looked like skyscrapers, seeming to go on forever.

"Did you get taller?" he asked, furrowing his brows as he tried to get the world to stop spinning around him.

"What?" she faltered, looking painfully self-conscious. Her cheeks burned, and she folded her hands over her chest. "Yeah, I grew like an inch or something." She shrugged.

"Cool," he said, pulling himself upright but stopping short of standing, knowing he couldn't manage a crazy task like that in his condition. Instead he scooted over to her bed and leaned against it, resting his head on the fuzzy blanket covered in cartoon kittens.

"I'm serious, Reid, I want you to tell me right now why you're drinking. Ever since you made the varsity team and started hanging out with all those idiots, you show up here drunk all the time. You've got to cut this out before you get in trouble." Her voice was sharp, but he still loved to hear it. There was something familiar and warm about the way she reprimanded him. A reminder that he was somewhere he could crash, give in to the whirling feeling in his head, and truly let go. Even if she was mad.

"It's fun," he said, slapping her leg playfully with his floppy drunken hands. "You should try to have some fun now and then. You just stay stuck in this room reading your books, playing that broken keyboard, and hiding out."

"Don't pull that on me," she lectured, kicking at him harder than he had expected. "I'm being serious. This isn't you. So why do you keep doing it?"

"How do you know this isn't me?" he snarled, shooting her an angry look. Tara didn't understand the pressure he was under. His parents had all these expectations for his future. The teams he played on demanded so much of his time to stay competitive. The friends he'd made wanted him to be like them. There was *nothing as comforting as someone else making the same mistakes as you. He could say: I'm not the only one screwing up. I'm not the only person failing. And in that camaraderie came comfort.*

Like the buzzing of a pesky fly dead set on landing on your sandwich, Tara wouldn't relent. "I know you so well, you don't need to answer the question. I already know why you're doing this. I only wanted to hear you say it. But I guess you won't." She flopped down onto her bed and pulled her knees up to her chest, pouting at him. She looked too big to sit that way, too grown up to pout.

"Let's hear it then, if you're so smart. Why am I plastered right now?" He'd spun so he could see her, his chin resting on her bed as he stared at her, like a puppy waiting for a scrap of food. He refused to admit he was afraid she might get the answer right.

"Because all these new people in your life keep telling you that you need to be more. You need to be faster and cooler and more fun. They keep telling you in not so subtle ways that you, just regular old Reid without the alcohol, without parties, without getting in trouble, aren't good enough."

He knew his face was ghost white now; he could feel the rush of blood whooshing away from it as a cold sweat overtook him. Maybe it was the tequila finally catching up with him, but he knew better. It was the truth that was making him sick. Spoken out loud, it was like being struck in the face with a hammer.

Tara slid off the bed and sat next to him, grabbing his chin and forcing him to look at her. "You are enough, Reid. You are more than enough. They measure things the wrong way. They don't see that you're the kid who stopped when the bottom broke out of that woman's

81

grocery bags. You were there chasing oranges around the parking lot for her. They don't see that you're the guy who always buys my lunch. How could they know that you feel people's pain so deeply that sometimes you don't know what to do with yourself when someone else is hurting. You need to stop feeling less than them. You are more than them. Miles more."

Reid reached up and took her hand from his chin and held it in his for a moment. Tara had always been caught somewhere between one of the guys and his little sister. At some point he started to grow taller, but she started to grow smarter, more insightful, mature. He'd gotten all the inches, and she'd gotten all the wisdom. He noticed for the first time the roundness had left her cheeks and she'd done something different with her hair. Her bright sea blue eyes were glazed with tears. When Tara cried it was like his insides were being pulled out of him and stomped on.

"Your hair is down," he said coolly, as though she hadn't poured her heart out to him. He grabbed a few loose strands of it and tucked them back behind her ear. "You always have it up in that ponytail thing."

"Just pass out already," she said, attempting to shove him back, but he didn't move. "At least when you're out cold you don't talk so much."

"No," he said, grabbing her wrist. "You're right. I don't know when you started getting so smart about everything, but you're right. I don't want to keep doing this." He gestured down at his body as though the alcohol had changed him into a different being. One he didn't want to be. "My shoes are on the wrong feet," he groaned, that seeming to be the best example of what a mess he was.

She broke free of his grip, but only because he'd allowed it. Tara moved down his body toward his feet and unlaced his shoes, yanking them free. "Your feet stink."

It bubbled up inside him, born out of a tiny laugh that bloomed into tears. He crumpled his face, trying to dam it all inside. Feeling exhausted, like the world had grabbed hold of each of his limbs and kept yanking in opposing directions until he was flat, he let it all out. "This sucks," he gurgled and wiped with the back of his hands at his eyes. "It's like this ride, and I can't get off. I can't go back to the way things were before. You and me, it used to be simple. We had fun, right? It was fun, all the stuff we did."

"You can go back," she promised, hurrying over to him and clutching his shoulder tightly. "You just need to forget these people. These girls, Mary, Sasha, and all the others, they don't care about you. The guys from the team. They don't know you."

"I know," he said, angry at himself for the uncontrolled emotional outbreak, the arch nemesis of any teenage boy. Tears. "Never mind. I'm fine. I'm just drunk."

"You are fine," she said, leaning and patting his hair. "You're fine. Everything is going to be fine."

It was hard to imagine how a girl who'd never in her life been shown comfort or compassion from her parents, could muster this much of it. And so freely give it to him. On the nights she sat alone and hungry in this broken-down house, never knowing what the next day would hold, no one ever reassured her. His life was idyllic in its lack of outside excitement, so much so that he sought out the mess and the drama. Tara, on the other hand, had unavoidable levels of it. She didn't need to create any.

He stared at her face, the sudden newness of it. It was the most familiar thing in his life yet it was like he was seeing it for the first time. Gone was the girl who played cards with him on every rainy summer day. This wasn't the silly-faced child who laughed so hard she'd pee her pants every time he made that joke about their guidance counselor.

Reid had always taken care of Tara the best he could, but her problems weren't ones he could solve. "Tara," he whispered, the tears all dried now. She looked at him quizzically, probably wondering why his voice was so low and controlled. Before she could ask, he leaned in and pressed his lips gently to hers. He expected a shove backward, maybe a slap or a shout. What he hadn't expected was her lips parting and her tongue swirling into his mouth. He didn't think she knew how to kiss, let alone French kiss—and pretty damn well.

Reid's hand slid to her cheek and held her there, not wanting this to end. It was like connecting so many parts of his life all at once. His best friend, his biggest cheerleader, was now also the person making his heart thud with excitement and his body beg for more.

But there was a buzzing in his brain, a tiny voice that had been so quiet lately. Every time he put a bottle of beer to his lips, he silenced it. Every time he skipped a math quiz he silenced it. But right now, with his lips on hers, it was growing louder every second. If there was anything between them, anything real, it wasn't meant to happen like this.

Reid pulled back from the kiss too suddenly to seem natural, and too awkwardly to be interpreted as anything accidental. *"I'm sorry,"* he stuttered out into the small gap between their faces.

"No," she said, clutching one hand to his shirt. *"No, I wanted you to do that. Don't apologize."*

"We shouldn't do anything tonight," he cautioned. *"I . . . uh, the drinking."* He ran his hand over his hair and swallowed hard.

"Yeah," she said, looking reluctant, keeping her face close in case he changed his mind. *"You should sleep."* She stood, and he ached for how nervous she looked. She rarely acted self-conscious in front of him and now tonight, it was all she seemed to be doing, all hunched shoulders and arms folding over herself. She walked to her bed and grabbed one of her pillows, tossing it to him. Then she yanked her purple unicorn blanket off the chair, throwing that down too.

"I'm not going to drink anymore," he promised, pulling the blanket up over himself, making the best out of the hard floor and ignoring the queasy feeling in his stomach.

"Good," she said, crawling to the end of her bed and smiling at him. *"I'll remind you in the morning when you forget you said that."*

But he already knew he'd be gone by the time she woke up. He'd changed everything tonight, and maybe that would have been all right. Until he realized this was what she'd been waiting for. Tara had high expectations for him and failing was about the only thing he did consistently lately. Knowing now she wanted something to happen between them, that she was depending on it, made him more certain than ever that it never could.

Chapter Thirteen

"I'm going with 99.9," Willow said, dropping a stack of papers down on Reid's desk. "I have found no pattern or indication of any habitual drug use. Her coworkers never reported her as acting anything other than a little tired. She hasn't been to a doctor in a long time, likely because she doesn't have good insurance. But the few records she does have don't indicate any issue of drug abuse. There are no reports to Child Protective Services. And get this," she flipped open one of the files and pointed excitedly. "I spoke with three former friends of the boy's father, and they all confirmed she was never part of the circle. As a matter of fact, they'll testify that when she discovered TJ's addiction she insisted he seek treatment and kicked him out of the house for Wylie's sake. She continued to try to help him but never allowed him back into their home."

"Told you," Tara said, blushing in the doorway of his office. She knew she was intruding, this conversation not meant for her, but some vindication was nice. She wanted the pleasure of gloating just a little.

"Tara," Reid said pointedly as he closed the documents on his desk abruptly. "You weren't supposed to come in until ten this morning."

"I thought I'd see if I could make a coffee run for you guys, considering I don't have any other means of payment. But who cares about that? You heard the good news."

"It's out of context," Reid cautioned, and judging by the look on Willow's face she knew this wasn't as cut and dry as she'd hoped.

"Willow just told you she's basically one hundred percent sure I'm not a drug addict. Is that not enough for you?"

"I wanted a chance to talk with you in private about how this would affect the case." Reid glanced over at Willow who took the hint to leave. Without another word she bowed out of the room gracefully.

When Willow left Tara felt her heart begin to race. Something felt wrong.

"Sit," he said and his voice was far too gentle for her liking. He'd had no problem being stern with her every day since this started, why lighten up now? "Dr. Palanthry, the psychologist you met with, sent his report over today."

"And?" she asked, recalling how kind the doctor had been to her. He was so understanding of how hard it was to be a single parent on a fixed income. He listened to her long drawn out stories of the hard work it took to make her life better and how she often felt like a failure.

"He believes you may have some level of postpartum depression. There's a wide spectrum for the diagnosis but it's important to our case. I want to ask you some questions, and I want you to answer me honestly." He folded his arms and leaned in across his desk.

"Postpartum depression?" she asked, twisting a lock of her hair around her finger nervously. She'd heard of it before but didn't know enough about it to be either worried or insulted.

"Leading up to the night Wylie was found in the parking lot alone, how were you feeling?" He glared at her so earnestly it was making her mad. Where was all this newfound empathy coming from?

"I was fine," she snapped. "I mean, I don't know a lot about depression, I'll admit that, but I think I was doing all right."

"Your card was declined at the supermarket," he said. "You were down to your last thirty dollars."

The way he read the facts off the sheet of paper in front of him was grating on her. It was like being dissected rather than talked to.

"I put some groceries back. It's not the first time that happened. We always make do. Wylie never goes without if that's what you're implying."

"It's not," he said, raising his hands up disarmingly. "Willow was able to get a copy of the footage from the supermarket. Wylie seemed upset. He was crying; you had to carry him while you pushed the shopping cart."

"It was too late to have him out grocery shopping, but it was the best I could do that day. He was tired, that's why he was crying. It wasn't out of the ordinary. Nothing I couldn't handle."

"Does he throw a lot of tantrums? I see he has history of ear infections. Those can be really difficult to manage. Kids don't sleep well when they have those, right?" He ran a finger across the paper in front of him, making sure he was getting all his talking points right. It was patronizing, considering how little he knew about children. How little he knew about her child specifically.

"Reid," she asserted, raising her brows nearly to her hairline. "Stop with the lawyer nonsense and just talk to me. What are you trying to get at?"

"Did you leave Wylie there because you needed a break? Was it just too much?" His hands came together in praying fashion, laced fingers resting on his desk, trying to appear casual.

"What?" she asked, snorting out a laugh. "You think I just abandoned my son because he was tired and crying. If that was the case, I'd have done it long before that. What's your logic here? I was going for a walk around the block and accidently got high? I promise, Willow is on the right track. I'm not an addict, and my son throwing a tantrum isn't grounds for me to just leave him."

"Were you filled with despair that night?" he asked, boring holes through her skin with his intense stare. His eyes danced all around her face, waiting for her to flinch. "I want to argue that you were overwhelmed, alone, and suffered a temporary lapse in mental stability." The flare of his nostrils and the deep breath he drew in made her heart leap with fear. He hadn't had a problem saying what was on his mind this entire time and now suddenly he struggled. "I want to argue that you were trying to end your life that night."

Tara could see now why he didn't want to say it. "I don't know what to do with this anymore, Reid," she said, slapping a hand to her forehead. "I don't know what you want from me. It's like everyone is claiming to know me better than I know myself. I don't remember that night after leaving the supermarket. It's just blank."

"Which may actually help your case. Willow has been cataloging you day in and day out, and any jury would be sympathetic to how hard you've been working and not getting anywhere."

"Not getting anywhere?" she asked poignantly, the corners of her eyes stinging with the threat of tears and the lump in her throat getting too big to swallow. "I know my life doesn't look glamorous. I'm not a high-powered defense attorney. But Wylie and I are happy."

"That's not what I meant," he replied, quickly trying to take the punch out of his words. "Listen to me, Tara. I can present this new information to the judge and the district attorney. There's a chance the charges can be reduced. You could be back with your son much quicker this way. Misdemeanor child endangerment is easier to overcome in civil or family court because it doesn't involve the same level of intent or malicious neglect. It's for people who make mistakes, who need help and seek it. We need to create some checkpoints, some mental health intervention and a support system that's sustainable for you. But this could change everything. Think about Wylie."

"You want me to say I tried to kill myself?" she asked, her words broken with emotion. "I don't think I can do that. I can't go there and lie."

"You can't say it's a lie," he cut in. "You admit you don't remember what happened that night. If the prosecutor can't find any evidence of habitual drug use, then what other explanation is there? They'll know they can't prove their case, and they'll back the charges down. Isn't that worth it?"

"Worth saying I'm suicidal?" Tara cupped her hands over her mouth, the word seeming too bitter and unsavory to let out again.

"Better than being a drug addict," he argued, his voice raising a few octaves. "You have no idea how lucky you are that Willow stumbled upon this. Just think about it for a minute before you shoot it down completely."

She bit at her lip to force herself to do what Reid was asking. "What would we do next if I say what you want me to say?"

A smile accompanied by a look of relief cascaded over Reid's face. "We're about to enter the discovery stage of the trial now that the arraignment is over. That means the prosecutor has to share information and evidence they've gathered."

"Everything?" she asked, feeling like she was about to be stripped bare and paraded through the court when the day came.

"By law it's any information reasonably calculated to lead to admissible evidence. We'll get a good idea of what they intend to do in court, who they'll call as witnesses. Once we have that information I think we should present this new evidence and petition the court to reduce the charges."

"Sorry to interrupt," a small and unfamiliar voice called from behind Tara. "This was just delivered," a girl said as she handed an envelope over to Tara who took it, assuming this was some kind of mistake.

"It's for me?" she asked, but the girl was gone before she had the question fully formed.

"That's my assistant, Elise. She's kind of skittish. Apparently I don't give off a real warm and fuzzy feel as a boss. She's always afraid to knock on the door."

When Tara read her name across the front of the envelope she flipped it and peeled it open. "It's a request for me to relinquish my legal rights as a parent and allow the adoption of Wylie by the Oldens. They have a lawyer." She handed the paper over to Reid and hoped he'd tell her to rip this up and forget about it. It wasn't time for that yet. She wasn't ready.

"Damn," he muttered, slapping the document down on his desk.

"What?" she asked in a panic. "Can they really do this?"

"There are a lot of options for grandparents looking to assist in the care of a grandchild while the parent may have some difficulties. They can request temporary custody. If they're concerned about being able to make medical decisions for the child, they can up the stakes and seek guardianship. If that's granted the parent cannot seek custody again without petitioning the court. But they've gone right to adoption. They'd become Wylie's permanent legal parents and you'd be unable to ever request custody down the road. It's a lofty request and most family judges would never even consider this."

"They are a powerful family in this community," Tara said anxiously, biting at her nails. "Maybe they are pulling some strings or something. I know the head of their church is very influential."

"The sooner we can close this criminal case the better. I'll draft up a response to this request, and that will initiate a hearing."

"We'd go to civil court? We're not ready for that are we?"

"I don't really handle cases like this," he said, reading the paper again. "But let's cross that bridge when we get there. All we can do is focus on getting these charges reduced."

"I need some time to think about what you said," she sighed, raising a hand as if to stop him from making any assumptions. Tara hadn't decided anything yet. "I just need to process."

Chapter Fourteen

It had been three days since Tara had been informed about TJ's overdose and reality was still eluding her. She'd been holding out hope over the last few months that he could get clean and come home. This half-life she and Wylie had been living would be a thing of the past. But now as the alarm by her bed blared and the darkness of the early morning hours taunted her, she knew her fate was sealed. There would be no fixing what was broken.

Turning off the alarm, she rolled toward Wylie and lifted his tiny fingers to her lips. Like every morning she tried to kiss him awake gently to ease him into a day that would be anything but easy once they were up.

"Pumpkin," she whispered in his ear, "we have to get the newspapers to deliver." Her pillow was still wet from tears, but her eyes were dry. There was no time to mourn or sulk. The fridge needed to be filled with food and the electric bill needed to be paid.

Wylie's eyes were closed but he smiled as she kissed her way up his plump little arm. "We're going to be all right," she promised him, even though he had no idea of the magnitude of their daunting situation.

"Mumumum," he babbled, pulling her hair to yank her closer to him. She kissed his smile and laughed at the way he tugged at her hair again.

A second later he was snoring again, swept up by darkness and the need for a few more minutes of rest. She could understand. It was all she wanted too. Tara contemplated what would happen if she pulled the blanket over their heads and shut the world out. No work. No running around. They'd grab some stuffed animals and hide here as long as they could. Let someone else worry about the future. Let someone else deal with reality.

There are some things you know, but until you let your mind say them fully you have hope of ignoring them. TJ was the lucky one, Tara admitted to herself. She was the one who would have to wake early every morning, comfort Wylie every time he was sick, and find a way to keep going on her own.

"Mumumum," Wylie whispered again, lost somewhere between dreams and waking.

"Hey pumpkin," she said, kissing him again on his cheek. Maybe TJ was free of all the pain and the endless work, but he was also missing these moments of joy. "Mom's here. I'll never leave you. No matter how hard it gets. You will always have me."

Wyllie's little eyes popped open and he squealed a laugh that triggered a smile she couldn't hold back, no matter how sad she was.

"It's me and you kid," she whispered into his curls as she lifted him from the bed. "And I'm not going anywhere."

Chapter Fifteen

"You can't claim your son is all you want," Reid said as he circled the room like a vulture. His voice had a razor edge to it, and Tara looked worried but not deterred. That was the problem.

"He is," she argued, looking like she might stand but staying put as he closed in on her. "I want my son back, but I'm not willing to lie to get him. It'll blow up in the end; I know it."

"We already established that with your memory loss of the moments leading up to the event there is no way to say this is a lie. You can't remember your state of mind that night. It's a reasonable assumption, considering the circumstances, and it's your best shot. Willow, please tell her. Bond over the mom stuff or whatever, but *tell* her."

"Legally—" Willow started, but Tara boldly cut her off.

"I fully understand the legal benefits of me saying I snapped and walked away from my child that night. But I know my state of mind. If I were going to kill myself there would have been days, much harder days than that, for me to have done it. Nothing would be worth leaving Wylie there. I am all he has, and I would not check out on him. I just wouldn't."

"What do you want me to do?" Reid asked, tossing his hands up. "We've gotten most of the information from the prosecution regarding their case against you. It's cut and dry. They've got you leaving the store with Wylie, then the witnesses and timeline outlined in the police report."

"Where's their proof that I'm a drug addict? Where's their proof of what happened that night?"

He reached for her arm, slid her sleeve up forcefully and pointed to the bruise where the needle had been. "That's all they are going to need. That's all that twelve of your peers is going to care about. I'm not trying to prove you didn't get high; I'm trying to tell them why. I'm trying to give them a reason to understand the behavior. It goes to motive."

"I had no motive because I didn't do this," Tara pleaded, her face throbbing with the rush of anger.

"Enough," Willow cut in with a maternal snap of her fingers. "She's right, Reid. We shouldn't be pushing this investigation to the lowest common denominator of what might have happened; we should get the real answers. We can see from the discovery that the prosecution is taking these charges at face value. They're going to bring in the responding officers from both scenes, an expert witness on the impact of heroin use, and the witnesses who found Wylie. They haven't gotten as far as we have. They don't know she isn't an addict. So they are treating this case like a slam dunk."

"As it stands," Reid growled, "it is. And this defense was your idea, Willow. And a damn good idea at that. Why back out now?"

"I have ears, I can hear her. She's saying she is not willing to say she tried to commit suicide even though we are telling her it would help her case," Willow said adamantly. "We can walk through the steps of that night and piece together what happened. If they aren't going to thoroughly investigate, then we will."

"You have three more days here before you head home," Reid scoffed. "And are you honestly considering the fact that an investigation will go in our favor? If anything, we're lucky the prosecution isn't digging any deeper." His blood was boiling now, frustrated by the logic being used. There was this pesky thing called reality that they both seemed ready to ignore.

"How many times do you need to call me a liar, Reid?" Tara asked, her narrowed eyes fixed on him. "Willow doesn't even know me, and she's at least willing to help me find out what happened. Can't you do the same?"

"What else could have possibly happened?" he barked.

"I don't know. Maybe someone did this to me. Maybe I was attacked."

Reid didn't bother answering, he just plowed forward with what he had planned. "This petition from the Oldens for you to relinquish your legal rights to Wylie isn't going away. I've reached out to their attorney, and he was adamant that they will continue to pursue permanent legal custody of Wylie. He told me a hearing date will be set soon, and we could expect to be in front of a judge by the end of the month. I've set a meeting with a colleague of mine. She works in the family court and has agreed to review the case. She's supposed to have an assessment when she gets here in fifteen minutes. But I don't know that any of that matters if we don't address this first."

"Willow," Tara said, ignoring Reid's explanation. "How do you investigate something like this? Where do you start?"

"I've seen the footage from inside the grocery store where you were that night. But there was no footage in the parking lot where Wylie was found. None immediately around the area where you were found either. But there are only so many routes you could have taken from the parking lot. There is bound to be some ATM or other surveillance videos we could try to get our hands on. Then I'd go down to the area where you were found and look for more witnesses besides the few who found you. The 911 call was anonymous. I'd track that person down too. There's still a lot we can do to piece the night together."

"She's already been back to that area," Reid snipped. "The very next day."

"I went back to try to jog my memory, to try to understand what happened. I wasn't there for drugs."

"You're wasting time we don't have," Reid cautioned. "We could be building a strong legal case for your psychological state and how it impacted your actions. Just hear Kay out and then consider it."

"Fine," Tara shrugged. "Then hear Willow out and consider investigating further."

He didn't answer. Instead he just drew in a deep breath and rolled his eyes.

"You two are worse than my kids," Willow scolded. "Keep this up and I'll separate you. I'm getting out of here. I need to follow up on a few things. Please try not to kill each other while I'm gone."

Chapter Sixteen

"Thanks for coming," Reid said, greeting Kay warmly and gesturing for her to take a seat. "I know you're busy so I appreciate the work you've done on this." He glanced over at Tara and she got the hint.

"Yes, thank you very much." She knew she sounded stiff, but it was getting unbearable to show gratitude in her situation. She just wanted it to be over. If Willow was here, at least she'd feel like she had someone in the room who understood the ache in her heart. Right now Wylie's drooling face should be glued to her chest as she rocked him to sleep for his afternoon nap.

"No problem," she replied cheerfully, her soft-edged jaw and long dangling earrings all Tara could see from the corner of her eye. She could tell Kay was beautiful without even giving her a full on look. A woman of power. Well put together. Smelling like expensive perfume. "I just wish I had better news for you. The Oldens mean business."

"Doesn't everyone attempting to gain custody from a biological parent mean business?" Reid asked, and Tara took notice of how much gentler his voice was in the company of Kay. She wasn't sure if she should be grateful he was comfortable enough to yell at her or insulted that he saved all his respect for a woman like Kay.

"Actually, no," Kay corrected as she crossed her long legs and smoothed her bright red skirt. "Most people act on sheer emotion and in turn underestimate the process. But the Oldens are very familiar with the system and more importantly the system is familiar with them. They've been foster parents for almost two years now. They are prominent members of their church and seemingly ideal parents."

"They aren't his parents," Tara barked but then shook her head apologetically as she gathered herself. "I just mean that I'm his mother, and they can't take him because they have money and can buy him better things."

"You're right about that," Kay said, turning toward Tara and touching her shoulder gently. "In custody cases it's not a matter of who the child would have a better life with. They need to prove not only that they can provide and care for the boy, but that you cannot. There is precedence that the best interests of the child as a legal standard in determining custody is erroneous when applied to a dispute between a biological parent and a third party because it does not appropriately recognize the weight of your rights."

"Um," Tara said, squinting her eyes as she tried to understand.

"That basically means being a biological parent gives you more right to him than anyone else. If you are fit to care for him."

"I can care for him. I've been caring for him every day since he was born." Tara's eyes filled with tears, and she wanted to slap the cherry red lipstick off this woman's face. Though she knew the anger was misplaced, it still showed clearly in her expression. Kay,

100

however, must have been a professional at being the punching bag, because she never skipped a beat.

"It's normally the preference of the court that reunification stay in play for as long as possible. That will work in your favor. But custody cases are highly discretionary and at times there is a blatant abuse of that discretion. You have to prepare for that."

"So some judge could like them better and I could lose him?" she asked, stunned by the holes in the process.

Kay made a face that tried to be comforting, but it didn't work. "Now, the Supreme Court has stated in previous cases that the child's best interest will be served by living in a parent's home. However, if circumstances compel a contrary conclusion, the interests of the child should outweigh the natural parent's rights." Kay pulled a notebook from her small bag and flipped through her notes. Tara was certain the legal phrases weren't necessary but maybe just a show of Kay's intelligence.

"But are they trying to prove there are circumstances here that would cancel out my rights?" Tara asked through a choked voice, trying to boil it down to its simplest form.

"You can argue that the biological parent has a fundamental right in the care, custody, and management of her child, which is protected by the due process clause of the fourteenth amendment. However, the Oldens have compiled a strong case. They intend to bring in a substantial list of witnesses. They aren't limiting their points to the criminal charges against you right now. They're saying there is a persistent neglect of parental duties that are drastically affecting the welfare of the child."

"What are they citing?" Reid asked, and Tara took comfort in his growing anger. At least he could see how crazy all of this was. She could hear the sudden change in his tone of voice.

Kay bobbed her head back and forth as though she were giving it all ample consideration. "In my opinion they are likely overreaching. But sometimes if they dot all the i's and cross all the t's it won't matter. They've had Wylie meet with a psychologist, a new pediatrician, and an early intervention specialist," Kay said, glancing at her notes. "They've pulled out all the stops, and they intend to create a rock solid picture of what Wylie's life would be like with them. They've even enrolled him in a local preschool that focuses on early literacy and social competence."

"Can I see him?" Tara asked desperately, pained to think of Wylie being dropped off at some school and left with strangers. *More strangers.* "Can't I get even a few minutes to hold him and know he's all right?"

"He is all right," Kay assured her. "There are social workers involved with the case, and they are making sure he's settling in to his grandparents' home. But unfortunately the terms of your bail state you cannot see him. Reaching out to the Oldens would be a mistake, considering how adamantly they are pursuing custody. Any communication could be twisted and used against you."

"So are you saying I'm going to lose my child to them just because they've spent some money to get some professionals to say whatever they want?" Tara sprang to her feet and paced toward the window, her anger growing too large for this small office.

"If I'm being honest," Kay started and looked at Reid for support, "it'll come down to the judge. Some have been burned too many times when it comes to addicts, especially heroin. It's an epidemic right now, and the odds of getting clean for a sustainable amount of time are low. If you get a judge who is jaded and hears the compelling evidence from the Oldens, there's a chance they could act swiftly and terminate your parental rights. But the precedence is to give you the opportunity to correct or amend the issues raised in the Oldens accusations and be reunited with your child." She placed her notebook back in her bag and stood. "I'm sorry I don't have more time today to go over this. My recommendation is you create a comprehensive action plan that includes a better support system for you and Wylie. Focus on the criminal charges and getting that resolved or settled. You should know the Oldens are citing the fact that you refused treatment as a testament to your unwillingness to get clean. I'm not sure if getting drug treatment is still something you would consider."

"What if the charges were reduced down to misdemeanor child endangerment?" Reid asked, and Tara wanted to cut in, more than she wanted to know the answer.

"Is that on the table?" Kay asked, looking surprised.

"It might be," Reid answered, shooting a glance over at Tara, making sure she was paying attention.

"That would certainly be easier to argue in family court than being convicted of felony charges. If it's a viable option, I'd pursue it. I don't have time to take the case myself, but please call me if you want any input. I'd be happy to give my opinion."

She was halfway out the door, glancing at her watch before Reid rounded his desk to follow her out.

"I'll walk you down," he offered, his hand planted gently on the small of her back as they left. Tara got the feeling Reid and Kay were more than business associates, and that unsettled her. A woman like Kay was all wrong for Reid. He didn't need that kind of perfect.

Nagging fear flooded her; she fished her phone out of her pocket and dialed. "Willow, where are you? Can you come back and pick me up at Reid's office? I want to help with the case. I want to go back to where it happened and see if I can remember anything. The only way I'm ever going to get Wylie back is if I get these charges thrown out. I know it's impossibly hard to believe me, but if anyone will, it'll be you."

Chapter Seventeen

The memories did not come rushing back to Tara the way she'd hoped. The walk from the parking lot of the grocery store to the alley in which she was found felt completely unfamiliar. They took every possible route between the two destinations as Willow took note of any surveillance options that could be utilized.

"You wait out here, I'm going to go talk to this consignment shop owner and see if these are dummy cams. If not, the footage could potentially be solid, considering it has at least a partial angle on the alley."

Tara nodded and looked up and down the street, knowing she should stay put. But the night after her arrest she'd tried to come back here. She was sure something would make sense upon seeing it. But she never made it into the alley. Something had spooked her, a hobbled mass shuffling down behind the trash cans.

Now in the light of day nothing was moving. With an urgency driven by nerves, she crossed the street and headed between the two large brick apartment buildings. The police tape had been torn down, but fragments of it still clung to the dirty metal loops on the dumpster. She closed her eyes and drew in a deep breath, trying to engage any of her senses. But to no avail. Nothing about this was familiar.

"No cats," a gravelly voice echoed down the alley, sending Tara jumping backward and cracking her elbow against one of the walls.

"Ow," she whined, clutching her throbbing arm. "Who's there?" She scanned the piles of debris and looked for any sign of life. There was a rattling movement under a large blue tarp a few feet from her. She edged back from it slowly, her breath catching in her throat.

"No cats," the voice repeated as the tarp yanked back and a clump of matted gray hair sprung out.

"I'm not a cat," Tara forced out, shivering with fear.

The woman's face was now out in the light, her eyes squinting against the sharp rays of the midday sun. "Alive?" she asked, shuffling toward Tara, her blue tarp tucked below her arm. Three clicks and a whooping noise escaped the woman's wrinkled lips as her head twitched to the side violently. It looked like a demonic possession, and the hair on Tara's neck was standing straight up.

"Are you all right?" Tara asked, reaching a hand out and pulling it back quickly, unsure of how a touch might trigger the woman to be more upset.

"Alive? The dumpster didn't eat you?" She pointed a curled finger in the direction of the dumpster Tara had been found under.

"You were here?" she asked, looking at the pile of garbage the woman had crawled out of. "Have you talked to the police already? Has anyone else come by to talk to you about what you saw?"

"No cats," she replied, another twitch sending her knotted hair jumping. "No talking. No one talks to me."

"I'll talk to you," Tara said, trying to strip away the unease in her voice. "Can I get you anything? Are you hungry?"

"Feed the cats," she said, touching her stomach and smiling. "Hungry."

Tara yanked her bag off her shoulder and dug through it quickly. Since she'd become a mother she was rarely without snacks. Pulling out a squished granola bar, she unwrapped it and handed it over. "My name is Tara, what's your name?"

"Tara," the woman replied.

"Your name is Tara?" she asked, trying not to be affected by the woman's manic toothless smile as she shoved the granola bar in her mouth.

"Yes," she said, nodding adamantly, then clicked and whooped some more.

"What's going on?" Willow's voice cut in and sent the jumpy woman springing backward, pulling the tarp quickly over her head. Standing like a statue she attempted to hide in plain sight.

"This woman saw what happened that night. I don't think anyone else has interviewed her yet. She was right there behind that garbage and stuff. I think she lives there. We have to talk to her."

"Tara," Willow said quietly, "are you saying the woman with the tarp on her head who is apparently clucking like a chicken is a witness you'd like me to interview?"

"Yes," Tara replied directly. "She saw me under the dumpster."

"Miss," Willow started, looking skeptically at the heap in front of her. "May I ask you some questions?"

She was met with only silence as the blue tarp shuffled backward.

"No cats," Tara said quickly. "No cats allowed."

The tarp stopped abruptly and peeled back, exposing the watery blue eyes and red cheeks. "No cats," she parroted back. "Dumpster ate you."

Willow opened her mouth but snapped it shut abruptly, trying to take in the being in front of her.

"But it didn't eat me," Tara assured the woman. "See I'm right here. Do you remember what happened that night? How did I get under the dumpster?"

"He fed you to it," she said as though the answer should have been apparent. She whooped and croaked a few times, rolling her neck awkwardly.

"Who did?" Willow asked, finding her voice again. "There was a man here?"

"What was I doing?" Tara asked, stepping out in front of Willow. "Was I awake? Did he carry me here?"

"We need a description of the man," Willow whispered harshly. "Nothing else matters."

"Sleepwalking cat," she said, slumping her shoulders and head and moving like a zombie for a few beats. "Sleepwalking cat eaten by the dumpster."

"The man," Willow asked quickly. "What did he look like?"

"Vampire," the woman shrugged casually, "vampire."

"How tall was he?" Willow asked, holding a hand up at different points to try to get the woman's input but she batted the hand down.

"No cats," she muttered as she moved past them down into the street.

"Wait," Tara pleaded but the shuffle only grew faster as she moved away.

"No cats," she shrieked loud enough to freeze Tara and Willow in their tracks. There was no stopping the woman who was in the closest thing to a run she could manage.

"Let her go," Willow said, catching Tara's elbow. "It's not like we could put her on the stand. She's not stable or sane."

"Hey," a gruff voice rattled behind them. "You looking to score?" he asked just above a whisper now. "I've got anything you want."

"No," Willow said with a straight-backed confidence Tara never could have mustered in this situation. Spinning to see the owner of the voice, she was met with a wiry little man whose head was covered with a yellow bandana. Two inky blue tattoos of teardrops sat at the corner of his left eye. The point of his nose looked sharp enough to cut glass. His eyes resembled those of a rat.

"I gots everything," he sang, gesturing his hand wildly and then tapping his pocket. "It's three seconds baby, three seconds to rush." He yanked up his sleeve and tapped his veins with two fingers.

"No," Willow repeated and looked utterly unimpressed. "Do you deal here often? The overdose here," she pointed at the dumpster. "Were you here that night?"

"Which one?" he scoffed, bouncing up and down from his toes then back to his heels as though he could hear some music they couldn't. "There's about one a week here." He snorted a laugh and closed in on them. "You a cop or something?"

"You're supposed to ask that before you try to sell me drugs, idiot." Willow shoved him back and flipped something metallic out of her pocket. Tara had never seen a switchblade before except in the movies. But the way Willow was handling it, she was certain it was not her first time.

"I haven't used this in a while," Willow admitted as she backed the man up to the brick wall. "I'm out of practice. Which you would think would be a good thing for you. But really all it means is I might only get one shot, and I'll have to go for the jugular. Do you know how long it takes to bleed out once it's severed?"

She was not out of practice from Tara's perspective. The handle was split in the middle and she spun it over he knuckles, back and forth, making it dance before finally snapping it against her palm and pushing the shining metal blade closer to the man.

"What do you want?" he asked, putting a dirty hand up to his neck to protect it. "I don't know nothing."

"The girl they found under this dumpster," Willow said, pointing behind her. "You were here? Did you sell her the heroin?"

"Oh that girl," the man said, inching his way back. "Yeah, yeah, I remember her. Too bad. She was pretty. But if you're going to put that much in your arm you want to die. But it wasn't mine."

"What do you mean?" Willow asked, closing the gap he'd just created between them, moving until he was forced against the brick wall behind him.

"The needle. It wasn't one from this hood," he explained, still holding his neck. "There's this exchange program they run here, trying to push clean needles. I get mine there. We all do. That dead chick's needle was huge. Like a hospital needle or something. I don't know, but it wasn't something she'd buy here."

"Dead chick?" Tara asked, not able to stay quiet any longer.

"Yeah, she's dead right? She must be. She looked it."

"You saw her?" Willow asked. "Were you the one who made the 911 call?"

"Uh . . ." he stuttered. "My phone was dead. But the cops were already coming. I saw the blue lights coming, and I bailed."

"Right," Willow grunted. "What else did you see? Was there a man here?"

"Nah," he said, shaking the idea off. "Didn't see anyone. Figured she just came here to kill herself."

"I didn't," Tara cut in, pushing past Willow. "I didn't want to kill myself."

"You?" he asked, staring at her like she was a ghost.

"You saw me, and you were just going to leave me there?" she asked, her anger sending her skin into a prickly heat. "You kept walking? Selling this poison to someone else? Don't you know what you're doing to people? These people have lives, they have families, and you're destroying them."

"I'm not doing shit," he argued, seemingly emboldened by the barrier Tara had created between him and the shining blade of the knife. "I make people feel better. It's medicine. You know, girl. It's a rush."

Willow yanked her back before she could argue anymore. "Go," Willow demanded, pointing assertively for the man to leave. "Get out of here."

Like a rat fleeing a sinking ship his feet skidded against the dirty ground as he sped away. His head spun back toward them, making sure they weren't following behind.

"I'm going crazy," Tara said, crashing her back against the brick wall and tangling her hands into her hair. "I can't take this anymore. I want Wylie."

"I know," Willow said, leaning against the wall too, but stopping short of touching Tara. She could use a hug, some kind of comforting touch but it was easy to tell that was not Willow's style. "I can't imagine being away from my kids and not knowing when I'd be back with them."

"You have to believe me, Willow. I can't say exactly what happened here that night but I would never do anything to hurt Wylie. To think of him in the cold, alone. That's not me."

"We're doing the right thing," she assured as she gestured for them both to head toward the car. "Finding answers will help. You can get through this."

"I can't," she said, using her sleeve to wipe at her eyes. "I'm not like you. You," she cast a long stare at Willow, "you are so tough. What you did back there, I couldn't do." She stared at the knife as Willow spun it closed and put it back in her pocket.

"I learned a long time ago tough is an act. No one is really tough. We're all afraid of the same things, we all want to go home at the end of the day. The knife, it's just a thing I learned that helps get me home."

"I'm not tough, I can't even act it."

"Bull," Willow said as they hopped back into the car. "The unfortunate thing about having your whole life investigated by a person like me is you can't lie. I've been asking myself over and over again how you've managed to do this on your own for almost two years.

But then I realized I shouldn't be asking myself how, but why."

"What do you mean?"

"You qualify for state assistance. Welfare. But you don't receive any. You don't call a single friend to save you on the days where it's too much. You work and you mother and you do it completely alone. But why?"

"My parents were supported by the government their whole lives. They probably still are. They were able bodied people who'd rather smoke and grow weed than work. TJ and I were doing fine before the drugs. We had split shifts at our jobs so one of us was always home with Wylie. Things were tight, but we were surviving. After he died, I felt like I had to keep that going. I can work, so I do. I cut coupons and eat leftovers. I can make it work, so I do."

"Then you're tougher than I am. Even without a knife." Willow laughed and even Tara had to crack a smile.

"What happens if I never get him back?" Tara asked, speaking out loud the words that haunted her in every quiet moment. They lurked in the shadows of her mind, coiled like a snake waiting for a moment to strike.

"I've been destroyed before," Willow admitted, focusing on the road ahead as she drove away from the alley. "I've been dismantled, yet here I am. Nothing is final but death. You have to surround yourself with people who will remind you that as long as you have a breath in your body nothing is final."

"I don't have any people."

"You have Reid, and you have me." She twisted one of the bracelets on her wrist and cleared her throat. "I met this woman years ago, before my kids were born. She was a stranger, and now my kids call her grandma. On my darkest days, through some of my hardest cases, I call her. When Josh and I have something to celebrate, I call her. She's all the way in North Carolina, but we still call."

"And she helps you? Even from far away? What can she really do?"

"She reminds us we're all right," Willow said simply. "Betty doesn't let us wallow in sadness or get too confident in our successes. Life is always trying to knock you off your center of gravity. Betty is our balance. You need to find more people."

Chapter Eighteen

Reid hadn't had a decent night's sleep since Tara first called him. Maybe that's why he was being such an ass lately, sleep deprivation. "So you're both sitting here, trying to convince me that an insane woman and a drug dealer who will not go on record have given you some pertinent information to the case. I'm supposed to be excited that you had to pull a knife on a guy in an alley to get him to talk? You went out there looking for security camera footage and came back with nonsensical information that does us no good."

"Are you done?" Willow asked flatly. "Because right now you sound like my son when he doesn't get ice cream after dinner. And you keep your house here about as nice as he keeps his room, for the record."

"I . . . uh," Reid stuttered, not completely disagreeing with her. "I'd like everyone to be moving in the same direction. I want to make a decision about reaching out to the prosecutor and getting the charges bumped down."

"You heard the part about the needle," Tara argued, pacing around his living room. There was plenty of room to do so since the furniture was so sparse. "It wasn't something I'd buy in that area. It was unique. It's a lead. We need to at least follow and see where that takes us."

"No, we need to stop wasting time and move on," Reid argued.

"Move on?" Tara ground out angrily. "Move on from this case that's annoying you so much? I'm sorry this is inconveniencing you. It's my life."

"That's not what I meant," Reid sighed, flopping down onto his kitchen barstool and covering his face. "Don't play that card, Tara, like I'm the one making this hard. I didn't put you in this position."

"Neither did I," she said, drawing out each word for emphasis. "I didn't do this."

"Reid," Willow interrupted, her voice gentler than he'd heard it in a long while. "I have concerns about the validity of the charges." The statement was broad; it was vague but somehow he knew exactly what she meant. She wasn't saying his defense wasn't strong enough or the details weren't ironed out. Willow was stating she believed Tara.

"The witnesses you spoke to today could not have been credible enough for you to form that opinion," Reid challenged. "We've worked enough cases together. I know you're a hard sell."

"The footage," Willow retorted, not seeming pleased with being challenged. "I had multiple store owners provide me with their security footage. There was nothing."

"What do you mean?" Reid asked, his stomach tightening.

"There were three walking routes from the store to the alley. I covered all of them for the time period in question. She never walked by."

"Are you implying some sort of teleportation?" Reid scoffed.

"Forty-three cars," Willow said, narrowing her eyes. "That's how many cars took those routes. I think someone took her there in one of those cars."

"Which proves what?" Reid growled. "So she got in a car with someone. She didn't walk. A couple days ago you thought she was trying to kill herself. Now what? You think she was kidnapped. I don't think I know any drug dealers who like to share for free. She wasn't sexually assaulted. She wasn't robbed. There's no motive here for anyone else to have been involved."

"Could we maybe stop talking about me like I'm not here?" Tara shrieked. Tossing her hands up, she pushed her hair out of her face the way she used to when they were kids and he was making her mad. "I'm tired of this. I can't take the back and forth and the not knowing. I hate this," she stammered, her breath catching. For the first time Reid noticed the flush in her cheeks was gone. Her eyes blinked hard as she steadied herself against his desk. The scene felt very familiar, and it scared the hell out of him.

"Tara," he said, his voice sounding surprisingly frightened.

Her eyes rolled up and her body went limp just as Reid got to her. She fell into his arms, and his heart seized with worry in a way it hadn't in years. Tara looked so small, her head resting in the bend of his arm.

"Is she breathing?" Willow asked, pulling her phone from her pocket just as Tara gasped and her eyes opened again slowly.

"Tara," Reid whispered, putting his hand to her cheek as she tried to sit up. "Are you all right?"

"I'm fine," she said, waving him off as she got her bearings again. "I'm just tired."

117

"You need to see a doctor," Reid insisted, ushering her over to his chair. "We can call an ambulance."

"I fainted, Reid, I didn't fall out the window. I'm fine."

"Fine, no ambulance but at least let me take you to the hospital," he said, looking over to Willow for backup.

"No way. I don't need anything else on record, getting twisted around. I'm not going to the hospital. Can we please just drop this and go back to me yelling at you."

"Your favorite sport," Reid said with a half-smile. The words felt like they were from a lifetime ago, an argument between kids about nonsense. But this wasn't nonsense, and they weren't kids anymore.

"Josh is coming," Willow said sheepishly. "He knows me well enough to know I wasn't coming home until I saw this through. He and the kids are on their way. We were going to make a little vacation out of it. He can come by and check you out."

"He's a doctor," Reid explained.

"If it'll make you feel better," Tara sighed, attempting to stand and then thinking better of it as her legs gave out.

"Sit," Willow ordered maternally. "I just sent Josh a text. I'll meet him downstairs and then we'll switch off. I'll get the kids settled in at the hotel while he looks you over."

Tara put a tired hand up to her head and focused her eyes. "Willow, thank you so much. I'm sorry for all the trouble this has caused. Your help, it means the world to me."

Reid couldn't accurately describe the look that passed between the two women. It's what separated him from the people in his life. This knowing, wordless communication, a language everyone but he seemed fluent in.

"Josh will take good care of you. Just sit tight. I'm going for a walk and making a few phone calls." Willow backed out of the room quietly, leaving behind a heavy silence.

"I'm sorry for raising my voice," Reid apologized, trying to focus in on every little twitch and change in her face, making sure she was all right.

"I'm sorry for dragging you into all this," she said in a whisper, blinking hard again and trying to focus. "You've got your life together, your career, and I bring my mess around. Just like I always did."

"You?" he scoffed, thinking back to every time he climbed in her window and tried to sober up. "I did my share of messing up your life."

"Is that what you think?" she asked, rubbing at her eyes. "You think you ruined my life? It was a little more complicated than that."

"I'm not sure it was, Tara. I can see my part in how things happened. I've never been able to forget it actually."

Chapter Nineteen

"Tara," an unfamiliar voice called through her screen door, and she considered staying hidden in the kitchen. "My name is officer Lincoln Smith and I need to speak with you."

A police officer at her door should have frightened her considering how much pot her parents kept in the house, but she didn't care. If they got caught it was their problem. Rounding the corner, she saw a man taking up nearly all of the door with his big shoulders and round protruding stomach. But he wasn't alone. In tow and looking completely disheveled was Reid. His eyes were fixed on the broken wood planks of her porch floor as she stepped outside.

"I need to ask you about last night," Office Smith continued, pushing his mirrored sunglasses up his nose. Beads of sweat were forming around his temples and racing down toward his chin.

"What about it?" Tara asked, still partly assuming this had something to do with her parents. Maybe they'd finally been arrested for something. But that didn't explain why Reid was with him.

She hadn't spoken to her best friend in nine days. Not since he'd kissed her and then disappeared. He didn't answer her calls to his house, and she took the hint. He clearly did not feel the same way about her that she did about him.

"Between the hours of nine and eleven last night, was Reid with you?" He gestured over at Reid with his stubbled chin.

"Yes," she lied. It came to her so quickly she knew it sounded convincing. "He got here before nine though," she continued, trying to look pensive about the timing. "There was a music video we wanted to see, and we were waiting for it to come on."

"And he was here until eleven?" Smith pressed.

She wanted to look over at Reid for some kind of indication of what this was about, or how she should answer but Tara knew better. Lies were in her veins recently. Her whole life was fake, and it had become second nature to say what people wanted to hear. Teachers asking why her parents had missed another teacher's conference didn't want to hear about their latest bender or how her mom had wanted to come but she'd begged her to stay home, knowing she was too high. That version of the story was too messy. So Tara would make something up. And the teachers, anxious to move on to the next pressing matter, would drop it. The same logic applied to worried neighbors and even Reid's parents. They all asked questions, but she'd gotten very used to the look of relief on their faces when she'd lie and let them off the hook. If Tara told them everything was fine, they wouldn't feel obligated to intervene.

"It was at least eleven. Probably a little later. I don't remember exactly. Why?" She now finally looked over at Reid who was trying to mask his astonishment. She'd covered for him without a moment of hesitation, even though he'd broken her heart.

121

"Are your parents home?" Smith asked, leaning over and peering through the screen door. She watched his nostrils flare and assumed the pungent smell of stale marijuana smoke was catching his interest.

"They aren't," Tara said, feeling the heat rise in her cheeks.

"Were they home last night, did they see Reid come over?"

"He uses the window," Tara said, pointing up to the lattice work. "But they weren't home anyway."

"So they aren't here now and they weren't here last night. When do you expect them to be home?"

"Not sure," she admitted through a smile, "probably tonight." She had no clue where they were or when they'd be back.

"I'll come back tonight. I'd like to talk to them."

"I'm fourteen you know," she said quickly. "I can be home by myself."

"For a reasonable amount of time I'm sure," he said, nodding his head. "But I'd like to chat with them anyway." He turned toward Reid, who was still staring at his shoes. "Just because you have an alibi now doesn't mean you're off the hook. I know you hang around with all those boys on the team."

"He hangs around with me too," Tara challenged, worried what might happen to Reid if she weren't more convincing. "I called him last night. I don't like to be here alone. I know he had other plans, but I pestered him until he came."

And like an ice cube in the sun, the man's brashness melted away. His robust voice leveled off and his squinting eyes relaxed. "I have to get back to the precinct," he said through a long breath. "You need a ride back to your house?" he asked Reid.

"I can walk," Reid said, speaking for the first time since he'd come up her steps.

With a nod and a gruff rumbling noise from his throat Smith stepped down the stairs and headed to his car. He took one more long look over his shoulder, appraising the disheveled state of her house.

"You can come in until you're sure he's gone if you want," Tara said with a shrug, trying to downplay the weight of the moment.

"Tara," Reid edged out, his eyes wide and unblinking. "You just lied to the police for me."

"My parents have basically been training me to lie for the last few years. It's no big deal."

"It's a very big deal. Don't you want to know what happened?"

"Sure," she said, falling casually on the porch swing as it creaked loudly under her weight. "I figured it was something to do with those jerks you've been hanging out with. You were bound to do something illegal."

"I wasn't there," he said quickly, looking too apprehensive to sit by her in the swing yet. "I wasn't with them. They really screwed up, Tara. It's bad."

"Shoplifting?" she asked, looking unimpressed.

"They burned the Shipley's barn down, and it jumped to their car. Some animals were killed. A firefighter got hurt. It's really bad." There were tears in his eyes, and she could see him struggling to swallow.

"Why would you do that?" she asked, trying unsuccessfully to mask her horror. They'd spent plenty of time when they were younger climbing on hay bales and feeding the goats at Shipley's small farm. It was a nice

123

place, a strange sight so close to the city, but the owners never gave them a hard time.

"I didn't," he argued. "I was with them at the beginning of the night, but they were getting on my nerves. They kept trying to get me to do all this stupid stuff, and I was sick of it. All I could hear was you," he said and stopped abruptly.

"What does that mean?"

"That stuff you said to me," he admitted, finally sitting by her, but keeping space between them. "You were right."

She searched his face, not looking for truth or lies, but instead she saw the boy she knew before everything had changed. That boy, that chubby face, she'd be able to believe. "I think you'll be off the hook. Smith looked way more interested in why my house smelled like weed and my parents aren't home. I'm sure he's making some calls about them right now."

"And what happens when he finds something and they get busted?"

"I'll go live with my aunt. It's what I want anyway." She'd said that lie so many times she nearly believed it herself. Her aunt was all right, a normal lady or whatever, but it wasn't home. She'd been up for a few visits and there were no other kids in the remote area to play with. It was boring and lonely. But lately so was her own home.

"Don't say that," Reid said pathetically. "You can't move. I know you, you don't really want to. There's nothing to do up there, and you don't know anyone."

"Whatever," she huffed. "The important thing is no matter what happens you won't get in trouble for the Shipley's barn."

124

"I wasn't there," Reid pleaded again.

"Okay," she said, sounding exasperated. "I believe you. But you should have given me a heads up. How did you even know I'd cover for you?"

"I didn't," Reid sighed. "I figured I'd get yanked out of here and have to go in juvie or something for a while. I just wanted to be able to see you first before it happened."

"Why?"

He looked at her with an air of annoyance that melted into a long stare she couldn't shake. "I'm sorry I left that night after we—" His lips snapped shut, and he looked unable to finish his sentence.

"It's no big deal," she lied, looking away. "I'm just glad you listened to me. You're better than those idiots."

"I don't feel much better than them. I treated you like dirt, and I'm sorry. You just put your ass on the line for me. You get the worst deal on things all the time, and you never complain. I shouldn't have blown you off like that." He reached his hand to hers, and she felt a heat roll over her entire body and land on her tingling scalp.

"Want to help me clean up the house for whoever that guy sends back here later?"

"Sure," he said, letting her hand go quickly when she didn't make a move to lace her fingers around his. "Aren't you worried your parents are going to get into trouble?"

"I think they might already be in some. They haven't been home in four days." She bit at her lip anxiously as she let this admission slip.

"What?" Reid asked, straightening up. "They've never been gone that long."

"I know," she croaked but then cleared her throat to get rid of the creeping emotion that was threatening to take over. "But I'm sure Officer Smith is on the case," she joked, standing up and heading into the house. "You owe me, so you have to clean the fridge. Lucky for you it's empty."

"Have you eaten?" he asked, stopping in the doorway and grabbing her elbow, forcing her to spin and look at him. He scanned her face in that lie detector way he always did.

"Not yet today," she said, rolling her eyes like he was overreacting.

"I've got cash. I'll order a pizza. Pineapple?"

"You never let me get pineapple. You hate it."

"You should have called me, Tara. I didn't know you were alone that long. I'd have come by sooner. They shouldn't leave you like that. It's not right. I shouldn't have left you either."

"I'm starting to figure out I'm pretty easy to leave," she whispered, staring up at the ceiling to hold her tears in place. "Pineapple," she smiled, finally gathering herself and looking at him.

"Yeah," he said, smiling that dimpled smile back at her. "Gross pineapple pizza."

Chapter Twenty

"Deep breath," Josh said, listening intently. She felt ridiculous sitting on Reid's one living room chair getting a physical. She knew the second his stethoscope hesitated on her chest that her cover was blown. "Have you been diagnosed with a heart condition?"

"She has a murmur," Reid cut in nervously. "When we were kids she couldn't take gym class."

"Thanks, Mom, I can handle this." She tossed him a dirty look and refocused on Josh who was looking concerned. "It doesn't cause me any problems."

"Do you see a cardiologist every six months?"

"Every six years is more like it," she laughed, but no one else seemed to find it funny. "I'm really fine. My heart isn't an issue for me."

"Normally, I'm sure it's not. Many people live their whole life without being bothered by a heart murmur. Most never require surgery or any intervention at all. But when you are severely dehydrated, suffering from sleep deprivation, and on the verge of being malnourished, it will certainly be tested."

"I'm sure Willow told you what's going on. It's been hard to sleep, and I haven't been hungry. I just want this all to be over."

"It could be permanently over, if you know what I mean. You need to take care of yourself. Stress isn't helping the situation either. You need help here, Tara, and I'm not talking about winning this case. Whoever you need to call, whatever you need to do, get some people to care for you. You need meals, rest, a friend to talk to. I understand what it's like to want to do everything on your own. I'm married to the queen of that kingdom, but everyone burns out. With your condition, it's more dangerous."

She pressed her lips tightly together and nodded obediently but offered no other expression of agreement.

"That's a convincing assurance," Josh laughed. "Reid, I'm putting you in charge then. Make sure she eats. Give her lots of fluids, something with electrolytes. No matter what, she needs sleep. I could write a prescription, but I'm not sure with the hearing you want any other meds or scripts floating around for you right now. Try some good old-fashioned remedies."

"Like what?" Reid asked, seeming overwhelmed by the challenge.

"Warm milk, soft music, read her a damn bedtime story if you need to. Just get her to sleep." Josh was packing his bag and pulling off his gloves.

"That's it? You're just going to go?" Reid asked in a sudden panic.

"Yes, because my wife is still working for you right now, and that's basically impossible with two kids in a small hotel room. And when Willow can't work she thinks of all the things in our marriage and life we could make better, and then I end up with a laundry list of things I need to do. So I'm going to take my kids out for pizza and a movie." His face was stern but changed quickly as his hand hit the doorknob. "Call me if you need anything else or if you don't feel any better by morning. I can come back anytime if needed."

"Thanks, man," Reid said, exchanging a firm handshake as Josh left.

"I'm really fine," Tara said quickly before Reid could make too much of a fuss. "I'll have something to eat and head home. I just want to get through the next days and hopefully Willow finds something we can use."

"Can you please stop?" Reid asked, moving toward the kitchen. "You're as stubborn as you were when we were kids. I know you're hungry, and I know you're worried as hell. So we're going to do what Josh said. You're going to eat, and talk, and rest."

"Maybe we could go over the family court stuff again. I feel like there's more there that I can give you answers to. So I'm ready for whatever they think they are digging up on me."

"Stop," he groaned. "I don't have any food here. But we can order something."

"No, you don't have to do that. I'm not picky. Whatever you have is fine," she said waving him off.

"It wasn't an exaggeration. I literally have nothing here that qualifies as food. And the only things I have to drink are tap water, which comes out orange, and alcohol." He pulled open the fridge as proof.

Tentatively getting to her feet, she shuffled uneasily toward the kitchen. "Reid," she laughed looking over his shoulder into the empty fridge then glancing around the apartment, "besides the lack of marijuana, this is basically the house I grew up in. Why are you living like this?"

"I'm hardly ever here. It's not that bad." He shrugged it off as he closed the fridge and looked around for something that would defend his point.

"Did that used to be a plant?" she asked, pointing over at a dead twig in a red pot on the window sill. "This is really sad. You must be making enough money at work. Tell me for real, why do you live like this?"

He made some indecipherable grunts, shuffling through the kitchen drawers for some take out menus. Not answering her questions, he put his phone to his ear and began placing an order. "Can I get a large pineapple pizza, extra sauce, some breadsticks, a meatball sandwich with extra cheese, and a Greek salad no olives, but add roast chicken. I'll take four bottles of water and a couple bottles of apple juice if you have them."

When he got off the phone she knew she should have wiped the starry eyed look off her face and gotten herself together, but she couldn't. For every moment he'd pretended their roots were small and unimportant, he'd just shown her how much he remembered the tiny details that made their history real. Reid had ordered dozens of pizzas for her when they were young and her parents failed to feed her. She'd ask for pineapple, and he'd hardly ever get it. Something they argued playfully about for years.

"You can crash in my bed tonight. I'll take the floor. If you're feeling better, and you still want to talk in the morning, we'll go over the family court stuff. But not tonight. I don't want to talk about the case at all."

He gestured to the two barstools, and she took a seat.

"What do you want to talk about?" she asked, propping her tired head up on her palm. "Politics, religion? Something fun like that?"

He tapped nervously against the counter as he sat down next to her. "Did you believe me about the barn? When I told you I wasn't there and you covered for me with the cops, did you really believe me?"

"No," she admitted with a breathy laugh. "I knew you were lying." Tara looked away, feeling terrible for the truth she was finally sharing with him. Reid could never stay quiet when an injustice was taking place, so if he'd really been wrongfully accused no one would have been able to shut him up. "But I also knew you wished you weren't there. You were riddled with guilt, and I wasn't going to push you into telling me the truth. It wouldn't have changed anything."

"It's one of the biggest regrets of my life," he said, clearing his throat. "Those other guys, they got in deep trouble, and I could have ruined my whole life with that one stupid choice. I really didn't start the fire; I didn't do anything, but I was there. I should have stopped them. If it weren't for you, I wouldn't be where I am today."

"Where you are today? In this glorious mansion with all the latest technology and all the food one could desire?" she teased, trying to lighten the burden that was crushing down on him. It wasn't completely clear if that mistake years ago had set him on this path of self-loathing or if there had been many after it that compounded his anger at himself. Regardless, no one could argue that his life today was a result of choosing unhappiness.

"You know what I mean," he shot back. "Those were very serious charges against me, and if you weren't as convincing as you were that afternoon with Smith, he'd have kept trying to prove I was there."

"I'm shocked the other guys didn't turn on you. They weren't a very loyal bunch were they?"

"They weren't," he sighed, leaning his arm on the kitchen counter and facing her. They both looked exhausted by life. "But they knew I hadn't really done anything besides stand there. They were probably afraid the police would use me as a witness rather than try to convict me too. They didn't bring my name up, and I never said anything about who did what."

"That's not what this is, you know?" she whispered, biting at her nails nervously. Reid was so intelligent it was hard to figure out if he was speaking from the heart or trying to lead her somewhere without making it obvious. "I'm not asking you to look at some cop and unblinkingly lie for me. I'm not asking you to believe me just because you don't want me to feel bad. We were kids back then. This is real life now. I've been asking you to remember who I was back then and that's wrong. I'm not that kid anymore. I didn't follow in my parents' footsteps. My son has never had to wonder where I was or when he'd eat his next meal. I provide for him; I show up for him. I'm not them. And now he's in a strange house wondering where the hell I am, and I have no idea if I'll ever get him back and—" Her breath caught in her chest as the blood once again whooshed from her cheeks. She could feel his hand on her arm, but it didn't do enough to ground her back to the moment. Her heart fluttered, and she knew she was about to pass out again. His light grip on her arm changed to a wildly tight one around her whole body as the world went black.

Chapter Twenty-One

Reid was surprised, with a job like his, that this feeling of helplessness and fear didn't haunt him constantly. Surely with the billions of people on the planet it wasn't just Tara who could make his throat close with worry, or his eyes sting with held-back emotion. Tara was a piece of him, implanted deep in his soul.

It should have dulled over the years they were apart. It should have eroded with time like the sand dunes at the quarry they used to climb. They slid away with rain and time and grew smaller beneath their feet as he and Tara grew larger.

They climbed them weekly no matter how many times his mother begged them not to. Some kids in some far away part of the country had died when a section of the sand had broken loose and buried them alive. It was all his mom talked about for a month. But it never stopped them from treating the place like their own playground.

That was the thing about being young, though. That reality, the knowledge that children had been crushed and killed by sand, wasn't enough to deter him from climbing the dunes. It should have been. The way his mother begged and nagged him should have been enough. But youth is its own version of suffocating. It was the lack of air getting to the part of your brain that controlled judgment and common sense. Every minute, every choice could be your last, but you never knew it.

Right now, with Tara draped in his arms like a ragdoll, he could finally understand the bone-deep worry his mother must have felt. Guilt filled him as he considered how many times he ignored her desperate pleas and did whatever the hell he wanted.

Tara stirred as he laid her gently on his bed. "Tara, wake up. I'm sorry."

"Stop apologizing," she managed through her faltering voice. "You have nothing to apologize for."

"I've got plenty," he argued, lying beside her. It should have felt strange, unnatural, but lying next to her was the most normal thing he'd done in a long time. It's how they watched monster movie marathons at her house every Friday that first summer they met. It's how they lay after that first night he finally asked her where her parents were all the time, and she told him how scared she really was to be alone.

"The pizza will be here in a few minutes. No getting worked up until you've eaten and had something to drink." He rolled on his side, propped his head on his hand and waited for her to do the same. That was how they used to talk, inches from each other, sitting in the dark so anything they said could get swallowed up by the night.

"Did you know I loved you?" she asked, rolling just as he hoped she would and facing him. But the question was unexpected.

"What do you mean?" he stalled, employing his courtroom tactics.

"Before I left, did you know how I felt about you, or were you oblivious? I know back then the two years age

134

difference probably felt like a lifetime of difference. You saw me as a little kid."

"For a while," he admitted, so grateful the darkness of his bedroom created a shield to hide behind. "But that changed. You changed and I saw you differently."

"But did you know I loved you?" she pressed.

"Yes," he edged out against his better judgment. Maybe this would upset her and she'd be overwhelmed again. But she deserved the truth. He'd been holding it captive all those years, and it wasn't fair to her. "I think I knew toward the end, the night I kissed you."

"And that's why you were gone when I woke up?" Tara asked, sounding as if lying down was helping her regain some of her composure. "You didn't feel the same way, so you left."

"That wasn't it," Reid said, letting his mind search for the truth he hid from himself. "I did care about you, and that kiss . . . it meant something to me. I was just scared. No one ever got me the way you did, and I thought everything would change. I didn't want to lose you. I didn't want to let you down and that was all I felt capable of doing. I was being a screwup and no one deserved that less than you did."

"Everything was changing already," she whispered. "I was already losing you."

"I'm sorry," he said, aching at the memories. He could recall every time he blew her off to do something with a bunch of people who didn't give a damn about him. "I was an idiot. And then when I needed you, you were there. But look what it cost you. If I hadn't gone to your house that day, if that cop hadn't been paying attention to the house, you would still have been around. I'll never forgive myself for how that went down."

135

"You really think all of that was your fault?" Tara asked, a spark back in her voice. "It was going to happen sooner or later. I was actually relieved when they took me away."

"You were?" he asked, remembering the look in Tara's eyes when the car from Child Protective Services pulled into her driveway. "It didn't look like that when you were leaving."

"It was just the shock of it," Tara explained, trying to make him feel better. Her attempt was transparent. "But it was the right thing. I couldn't keep going that way. I was alone all the time."

"But the way things went after that," Reid said solemnly. "I tried to get in touch with you. But you never called me. I couldn't track you down. Why didn't you ever call me?" His rising voice gave away his hurt, the complete confusion he'd built up over the years.

She drew in a deep breath, clearly choosing her words carefully. "My life would never be the same, and I didn't want you to have to deal with that. I figured you'd be mad, but you'd get over it. If you knew how things really happened, you'd blame yourself no matter how I tried to convince you otherwise. I didn't want you beating yourself up over something that wasn't your fault. I guess maybe you did anyway."

"I just figured you went with your aunt like you said. I thought you were pissed at me, and that's why you didn't call. When I finally tracked her down in New Hampshire, it was the first time I realized something was wrong." Reid remembered knocking on the door of the old cabin in the woods fully expecting to find Tara there. He'd built up this image of her in his mind. Tara was busy reading books and swimming in the lake, probably making tons of friends in her new school. She was never alone anymore. He was sure of it. When the door had opened and he heard Tara had never made it to New Hampshire, his stomach had flipped and his palms had begun to sweat.

"My aunt had gotten married to someone after a few months of dating, and he wasn't very fond of kids. Children services called and she wasn't interested in becoming my custodian." He was amazed how matter-of-factly she recounted what must have been a crushing reality at the time.

"And you went to Texas?" he asked, imagining how frightening it must have been. "Your uncle or something? That was the most I could get out of your aunt. She didn't want me there."

"That makes two of us." She laughed, and it clawed at his heart for her to joke about it. "He wasn't really my uncle," Tara explained. "He was my great aunt's second ex-husband. She'd died the year before. I'd met him once when I was little. I think he was third or fourth on the list, but he had room for me and everyone seemed satisfied it would keep me out of foster care."

"How . . ." he stuttered nervously, "how was it there?"

"Fine," she chirped, too pleasantly to be telling the truth. "I stayed out of the way. Worked a thousand hours a week at the local ice cream shop and saved enough to get out of there when I turned eighteen. I made my way back to Boston and started working here. After a year or so I actually had the stupid notion that I could go to college. But it didn't turn out that way. TJ and I met, and six weeks later I was pregnant."

"I would have come for you," Reid said, his eyes trying to focus through the darkness so he could see her face. The edges were there, but she still felt far away. "If you would have called me, I'd have gone to Texas and gotten you. I don't care what it would have taken. I know you're making it sound better than it was down there, and I wish you'd have reached out to me then. I thought about you all the time, and I just imagined you were so angry with me."

"I wasn't angry with you," she said, and he could sense her smile. "Maybe I was angry with the world, with fate, but I was never angry with you. I kept loving you the whole time."

"Then why didn't you call me? You knew I'd be there."

"I think that's why I never called. I was convinced my life was this vortex, and I'd suck you in and ruin the chance you had at being happy. You don't have to admit it, but think about what your life would have been like if you had to come rescue me."

"There were ways we could have made things work," he sighed, knowing she was probably right.

"Even when I returned, I knew you were off living your life. You were far easier to keep tabs on than I was. I knew you graduated and went to college. I asked around about you, and Pepper Roosevelt said you were dating a girl named Lulu. She said you'd brought her to some parties back in town and everyone loved her. You loved her."

"I thought I did," he cut in, remembering Lulu's short blonde hair and sparkling white teeth. "She was a nice girl but I didn't love her."

"Why not?" Tara asked, genuinely sounding interested in the answer.

"It was too easy to be with her," he admitted, thinking back to the way Lulu agreed with anything he said. She was never put out by a mistake he made, never overly critical of anything he did. "I didn't have the right words for it then, but she was an enabler. I'm always halfway down the slide to hell, you know that. I'm hanging on, climbing up, and the last thing I need is a woman who is willing to slide down with me. I hear myself say it, but my last ten years of dating has basically been the same thing. These women are all brilliant and kind, and they think I'm perfect. They expect me to be and inevitably when I'm not, they keep pretending I am. It's a game and it usually goes on too long."

"That's sad," Tara huffed, fluffing her pillow a little. "Why do you keep doing it? Why pick the same kind of woman?"

"I think they pick me." He laughed. "I need someone like . . ." He paused, remembering this moment was bigger than just two friends lying in a bed. Tara was still in serious trouble and he was charged with helping her out of it. No sense in complicating things with the truth. "I need someone who tells me I'm an idiot and jerks me back where I belong. I need to be held accountable when I'm sinking."

"You and Wylie are the only people I've ever really loved," she admitted, sniffling now. He could hear her wiping her cheeks and trying to compose herself. "I didn't know TJ long enough to really love him, and by the time I thought I could, the drugs had hold of him. Every single person in my life has treated me like I'm disposable, except you. You never did."

139

"I let them take you away," he said, seeing the flash of her face pressed to the glass window of the Child Protective Services car as it sped away.

"There was nothing you could do," she assured him, reaching her hand out and touching his cheek. Her fingers were cold and small. Reaching up, he covered them with his own warm hand and held them on his cheek. He wanted to pull her fingers to his lips and kiss them gently. But he didn't.

"You have to sleep tonight. Josh said so. I know you're tired. I should shut up and let you sleep."

"I'll sleep tonight," Tara hummed.

"Why are you so sure?" He let her hand go reluctantly.

"I've never slept better in my life than when you used to crash on my floor. I always gave you a hard time about it, but when you climbed in my window I knew for that night everything would be all right."

"I don't know if everything will be all right," he admitted, wanting to remind her how serious the situation was and how little control they had over it.

"I just need you on my team. I don't need you to use everything you know and everything logic tells you, I need your heart. I need my best friend, because if this doesn't work out, if we fail, you're the guy I am going to have by my side. All right?"

The doorbell rang and he felt her jump. "The pizza," he said, rolling off the bed. The timing had either been perfect or terrible, depending on if he wanted to answer her question. But she deserved at least that. "I'm on your team, Tara," he promised as he slipped out of the room. He realized he'd been confusing the issues. It wasn't a matter of whether he could fix everything for her or make this like it had never happened. There was a big chance he couldn't accomplish that. But it didn't mean he couldn't stand by her, be there for her, and help pick up the pieces.

Like the old days, when she was hurting, he'd do what he could. It wasn't about fixing her parents or making her life better. Sometimes it was just bringing her pizza, watching some terrible movies, and letting her know she wasn't alone.

Chapter Twenty-Two

The smell of bacon was powerful enough to penetrate the soft edges of Tara's dream world. The visions of Wylie's tiny hand in hers as he teetered toward the park vanished, and she groaned sadly.

"I thought you'd be happy for breakfast in bed," Reid said too cheerfully, obviously not knowing her simplest yet most profound joy had just been snatched from her again.

"I was dreaming of Wylie," she admitted as she scooted to a sitting position and pulled the blanket up over her. It had been fine for her to hang around in a long oversized shirt when they were kids, but now they were grown. Age did that to you, Tara found; it gave you more reasons to cover up, to hide.

"Are you feeling any better?" Reid asked, sliding a tray of food onto her lap. It smelled far better than it looked but as she dug in hungrily she found it tasted just fine. "I'm not much of a cook. I went to the store this morning while you were sleeping."

"You didn't have to do all that," she said with a mouthful of eggs. "But it is delicious. Thank you."

"I'm going to the Oldens' today," Reid said tentatively, knowing that would send Tara into a frenzy. "Before you say anything, you cannot come. I'm going to be discussing the civil case with them. I can't represent you in that case; I'd be doing you a disservice. It's not my area of expertise, but I can at least discuss it with them, try to get a better understanding of any room for compromise."

"What kind of compromise?" Tara asked, tightening her grip on the fork and tensing up. "I'm not going to make some kind of deal when it comes to Wylie."

"I wouldn't ask you to," he promised, tossing his hands up disarmingly. "I'm going to see what we're up against. Maybe they only want Wylie in their lives. Maybe they'd even be willing to become part of your support system. It's worth a conversation."

"You think you'll see him?" she asked, biting at the inside of her lip to keep the pain in her heart at bay. She tasted blood, waiting for his answer.

"I'm not sure. I'm meeting them at their home, so there's a good chance. I can't really tell him anything for you."

"I know," she nodded, her mind racing for some way to connect with Wylie even if she couldn't be there. "Just maybe if you see him, call him Pumpkin. That's what I call him." Her eyes went wide and pleading, but she didn't care how pathetic it made her seem.

"I will," Reid agreed, heading nervously for the door. "Willow is going to come by and pick you up in a little while. She said she's got a lead on the anonymous 911 caller. No clue how she managed that, but maybe you can make something of it together."

"Thank you for last night, Reid. For everything, really. I can hear myself. I know there are moments when I'm not sounding grateful. But know that I am. I couldn't get through any of this without you."

"You're so tough, Tara. I have a sneaking suspicion you could get through anything without me, but I'm glad you don't have to."

He stepped out of the room and a few minutes later she heard his car start in the driveway. It was strange to be in his home without him. The room was sparse. Just like his office, it was void of anything personal. His closet door, half opened, showed neatly hung clothes fresh from the dry cleaner and shoes precisely lined up on the floor.

Everything in his life seemed stripped down and in order. Her house was usually littered with crushed cereal or clothes piled high, waiting for the next trip to the laundromat, a task that never seemed convenient or easy with Wylie in tow. Fighting off envy of the simplicity of Reid's life, Tara reminded herself that he was missing out on so much. He'd probably never stepped on an unforgiving baby toy at two in the morning while trying to get a toddler to the bathroom before the toddler threw up on the floor. But he'd also never rocked a sick child back to sleep, forgetting how his back ached and his stomach rumbled with hunger. When your arms are the net that catches a child and holds him through his sickness, sadness, and fear, you can ignore the mess. You don't count the dust bunnies or worry over the spilled juice. Reid's life was simple but overtly empty, and nothing could make her trade places with him.

Chapter Twenty-Three

The Oldens' estate on the north side of Boston would have been sold short by the adjective *large*. Reid had, through his law firm, attended the dinner parties of former politicians, a Miss America finalist, and two moderate celebrities who he'd lied and said he had heard of before. Yet all their homes would have fit comfortably inside the Oldens' with room to spare. As he parked his car in the circular driveway and took note of the gardens to his left, he realized even with the size of the property and home, there was nothing particularly pompous about the place. The plants weren't showy and perfect; they looked like they were planted with care and chosen because they were favorites not because they all matched perfectly. The door, though double wide and mostly beautifully etched glass, was adorned with a small plaque that read, *All are welcomed, all are loved.*

By the door, shoved hastily to the side, were three pair of rubber boots covered in mud. They ranged in size like a perfect story book, a pair for papa bear, mama bear, and baby bear. He glanced over his shoulder as two men crossed the driveway looking worried.

"Can I help you," the taller of the two men asked, his hair all white, blowing in the cold wind. He pulled his coat closed and waited for Reid to reply.

"I have a meeting with Mr. and Mrs. Olden this morning," Reid explained, eyeing a second man he immediately pegged as either a police officer or some kind of security. He wasn't in uniform, but there was a readiness to him, his stiff back and skeptical scowl giving him away.

"Oh, you're Reid, right?" the older man said, extending his hand. "I'm sorry. This is Tony, a friend of mine from church, and I'm Mr. Olden. You can call me Todd. You'll have to excuse us, we were out dealing with a broken fence post on the back of the property, and I lost track of time."

"No problem at all, Todd. It's nice to meet you. And you, Tony." He extended his hand to the wide-shouldered man with the scowl and immediately wished he hadn't. His knuckles cracked under the pressure of the man's grip.

"Please come on in and meet my wife, Millicent. I'll be honest, we were surprised to hear from you, considering you are representing her." He swung the door open and waved them in, but Reid caught the unsavory note in Todd's voice as he said the word *her*.

"I'm not here today as her representative in her federal court hearing. I'm actually just wanting to talk to you and your wife about Wylie. I was hoping we could have some open dialogue about his future." Upon Todd's urging, Reid took a seat in the first room they came to.

"What about Wylie?" a tall thin woman with dark brown hair and matching tired looking eyes asked as she cut into the room quickly, a chubby child perched on her hip.

146

Reid shot to his feet. "It's a pleasure to meet you Mrs. Olden, and this must be Wylie," he announced, tipping his head politely.

"My friends call me Millicent; are you my friend, Reid?" There was pain and anger twisted in her face, though the forced smile she wore hid it partially.

"I'd like to hope we could have a friendly conversation, ma'am." He knew his way through traps. That was a skill a lawyer had to master. Answer the question without boxing yourself in.

"I told Todd not to take your meeting. Just so you understand which of us is welcoming you here. We're in the middle of a battle and fraternizing with opposing counsel is never a good idea. But we're trying to be godly. We keep our door open to those who knock. With that said," her sternness melted away slightly as she looked him over from head to toe, "what can I get you to drink?"

"I'm fine, ma'am, but thank you. I'm not actually going to be representing Tara in the custody case. That's not my expertise. I think it's important you know that."

"Right, so you're the defense attorney trying to get her off for the heroin thing?" Millicent asked, twisting her mouth as though she'd just tasted something bitter. She whispered the word heroin as if it would mean anything to Wylie if he heard it.

"That's why I wanted to come here today. I shouldn't share this with you, but I want the focus to be on Wylie and his future. With that in mind, I wanted to disclose that the standings of the felony charges are not strong. We've built a good defense, and I don't believe Tara is a drug addict or that she'll be convicted of felony neglect." It was a bit early to be calling the latter, but he

147

needed to appeal to the Oldens' reasonable side. It would be easy to want to take a child from a drug addicted mother, but if that wasn't the case, wouldn't they be more openminded?

"The case is not going to stick?" Todd asked, freezing in his tracks, hovering for just a moment over the chair he was about to sit in. The room had dozens of chairs, all arranged in little pockets for small groups to gather and chat. It was clearly the room you put people in when you don't want them going any farther into your home.

"And without those charges the only thing keeping Wylie from being back with Tara is your petition for custody. I'd like to talk with you about that. Maybe we can discuss and brainstorm ways for you to be in Wylie's life and provide more of a support role for Tara."

"I notice you don't call her your client," Millicent snapped. "We've looked into you; she can't afford your bill, so how exactly have you arranged this relationship?"

"Tara and I were friends when we were young. I knew her when we were children, and she called to let me know there had been some kind of mix-up and she needed help." Reid straightened his back as Tony, the security man, paced outside the sitting room. "I can assure you there is nothing unpropitious about our relationship. I am representing her because I believe she is innocent."

"A mix-up, is that what she's saying that was? How do you accidently do heroin?" Millicent scoffed and whispered the word heroin again, this time while covering Wylie's ears. "This is nonsense. We will not sit here and talk about reunification or any other agreements. Let the courts decide."

"Reid," Todd interrupted, now sitting with his legs causally crossed as he seemed to take in the situation from all angles. "We love Wylie. He's been out of our lives for some time but that hasn't changed anything. He's our grandchild and if you look around, and I welcome you to, you will see we are doing everything we can to provide him a happy, safe, and healthy environment. It's what we've done for dozens of foster children over the last couple of years. It's even more important to us now, considering he is our flesh and blood."

"I understand," Reid said calmly. "But the courts normally favor reunification. If you know the system, you know that. I'm not here to broker some deal or pull any strings. I'm just here to talk about a long-term solution that might be right for everyone. Including this little pumpkin." Reid winked at Wylie and watched his tiny ears perk up and a smile form as he looked around.

"I'm blown away that she isn't going to jail. What plausible argument can you make that she is innocent? She left this child out in the cold." Millicent's voice was in a whisper again as she discussed the details while Wylie played happily with a loud singing toy.

"I can't go into all the details but there is more at play here," Reid said, trying not to get off topic. "Would you both be willing to say if Tara is not a drug addict you would want her to have a relationship with her son? Would that be within reason?" He was starting low, hardly asking very much of them at all. But the gasping noise that came from Millicent was not promising.

"Wait right here. Tony, please take Wylie into the kitchen for a snack." She dashed out of the room as Tony came in and scooped the child up with a tickle and a monster noise. The boy squealed and shrieked happily, chirping the word *snack* as they walked away.

A moment later Millicent returned with a stack of papers in her hand. She slammed them down, mostly for effect he could tell, on the coffee table in front of Reid. "This is the information that has been provided to us from our lawyers and investigators for the custody trial. You seem like a reasonable man, a good man really. I'm sure in your line of work you are frequently stuck defending people who are just plain guilty. And a good man would struggle with that. Do you struggle with that?"

"There are cases," he began, but she cut him off before he could qualify his statement.

"Do you have a relationship with God, Reid?" she asked, tears forming in the corners of her eyes as she swallowed back her emotion. Her mascara streaked dramatically down her face as she cried.

"I think we're losing the reason for this conversation," Reid tried, but she cut in again.

"I'll take that as a no. Well, I do. And I cannot in good conscience lay my head on my pillow again if this child is placed back with that girl. I think you are a good man, so I believe if you knew the things on those papers you wouldn't be here. You'd never try to give Wylie back to her if you knew."

The pile of papers in front of him took on a life of their own. They were a twister, willing his hands to them, pulling him in. The lawyer in him needed to see what kind of case the Oldens were building against Tara. But the friend in him, the one who wanted to believe everything Tara had told him, was reluctant to look. As it had for most of his adult life however, logic trumped emotion. He lifted the stack and glanced at various documents. All were compiled neatly and court ready.

"She's shared with me about her babysitter. Tara told me she's young," Reid began, taking note of the first few sentences of the top sheet. "But girls of that age do babysit."

Millicent could hardly catch her breath as she struck with her argument. "Wylie touched the hot stove while she was babysitting. The little girl was cooking something on the stove. Ludicrous. And instead of taking him to the hospital for the burn the woman upstairs treated it. She's a dental assistant. Not a nurse. Not a doctor. He should have been taken to the emergency room. It left a scar for goodness sake." She gestured animatedly, pointing on her own hand where the scar was on the boy. She paced so quickly Reid had to snap his head around to keep up with her as she bumped from one elegant piece of furniture to the next on her way across the room.

Reid flipped a few more pages, trying to scan them as quickly as possible. "A neighbor found him wandering the hallway of the apartment complex?" he asked, looking at the list of names corroborating the story.

"Yes," Todd finally chimed in, but his voice was less accusing and more pained. "It was in the middle of the night. Some drunken man coming home saw him on the first floor, playing with a bunch of cans from the recycling bin. Tara was asleep."

"Or high," Millicent interjected coolly.

"Was it reported to the police?"

"No, the man knocked on all the doors until someone recognized Wylie, and they woke Tara up. Think about what might have happened if the wrong person would have found him first. Or if he'd fallen down all those stairs. It's a terrible neighborhood she lives in. Have you seen her apartment? It's squalor. Uninhabitable. There are pictures." She pointed at the stack and urged him to look.

Reid picked up photos in crisp colors, like those taken by a real estate company in an effort to sell the property quicker. But instead of highlighting the magnificent features of the place it homed in on the disarray. There was a stack of laundry overflowing two hampers. The bed had broken, and slanted sharply to the left. Dishes overflowed in the sink and piles of droppings, probably from a rat, were photographed as well. It wasn't quite a house of horrors, but the photos told a story.

"He was covered in bites," Millicent said in hoarse whisper. "Some kind of bug. Bedbugs, I'm sure. There's more, plenty more for you to see. Just look at the notes from her pediatrician." Reid skipped ahead through some papers and found what she was talking about. "He has been pushing her, when the girl bothers to show up for appointments, to schedule Wylie for surgery for his ear infections. It's a simple procedure with tubes. It'll stop all his suffering, but she can't be bothered. They even have records that she hasn't been filling his prescriptions for the antibiotic. She just lets poor Wylie's eardrums burst."

"I think it's honorable you came here today, son," Todd said, standing and stuffing his hands in his pockets. "This isn't what you were expecting to hear, I'm sure. But now that you have, I hope you can see why we're going to fight so hard to keep Wylie here with us. And maybe rather than focusing on convincing us we should help Tara, you should convince Tara she should help Wylie."

"She doesn't deserve a thousand chances at his expense just because she gave birth to him. There's a story in the Bible; I'm guessing you haven't opened yours in a while." Her unnatural penciled-in eyebrow sprang up judgmentally. "I don't challenge the good book very often, but maybe you've heard of the judgment of Solomon."

"Cutting the baby in half," Reid replied smartly. It wasn't because he'd spent his life in a church but because the story had been brought up in one way or another in more ways than one would imagine in the modern day courtroom. It was meant to be some kind of example of infinite wisdom of an impartial judge.

"Yes," she replied unimpressed. "I don't intend to tell the world to give Wylie back to his mother just to keep him in one piece. Considering how she's mothered him over the years, I think it's just a matter of time before he's gravely injured. I will fight for this boy. I will use every penny and every contact to make sure he stays with us. We will hire the best lawyers; we will do whatever it takes to keep him from her. It's not because we feel he can have a better life here. It's not because we are selfish and want him all for ourselves. It is simply because we don't think he stands a chance with her. And if there is even a part of you that believes the same thing then shame on you for helping her."

"Millicent," Todd scolded. "The boy is just trying to—"

"No," she snapped back, waving a hand at her husband angrily. "No, I know it's part of your job to sit next to people, bad people, and try to gain their freedom. Even if they don't deserve it, even if you know they are guilty and they might reoffend. That's what you get paid to do. I'm looking at you and I see it. I see it in your eyes. You're tired of it. You are sick about it. So stop. Stop fighting for the wrong side."

Reid felt violated in her assessment of him, in the accuracy of it. "I should go," he asserted, standing quickly and already halfway across the room.

"I'm sorry you had to find out this way," Todd apologized, mopping sweat from his forehead and seeming to ignore the tiny hum of protest from his wife. She clearly didn't agree with his take on the situation. "You're a good man for coming here, and we too have been shocked by how bad this really is. If we had known, we would have acted sooner. But now that we do know," he said, extending his hand for a shake and waiting for Reid to take hold before he spoke again, "we can't turn a blind eye to this."

"Sorry for the intrusion," Reid said with a dodgy glance out the opened front door. "Have a good, um, I will just . . ." He let his words trail off and hurried down the steps and out to his car. He'd heard the expression *seeing red* before. It had actually come up in court plenty of times. A defendant's excuse that upon learning or witnessing something they were so overtaken with emotion or anger that their senses were washed with a blinding red hue. For the first time Reid could not dismiss the notion as some lazy excuse for lack of self-control. Because as he slammed his car door shut and forced the key into the ignition everything in front of him was a hot red cloud. There was so much she'd left out, and he had let her do it.

Chapter Twenty-Four

"This guy's a tweaker for sure," Willow said as she wrapped her scarf around her neck and leaned against the brick wall of the pharmacy, waiting impatiently for Tara to hand over her coffee.

"I spilled half of it on the way here," Tara admitted sheepishly. "I was shivering to death." The words were like a cork in a bottle, plugging up her throat. The thought of Wylie shivering in that dark parking lot alone flooded her the way it always did when she forgot to push the vision out of her mind.

"It's fine, I hate coffee anyway. It's a necessity, not an indulgence, for me," Willow admitted, folding her hands around the paper cup and letting it warm her slightly. "I need something to do while we watch Dante Yule doing a bunch of nothing."

"What exactly are we hoping to find by standing over here and watching him?" She squinted to see better across the street and try to make sense of this stranger's weird mannerisms. "What exactly is he doing?"

"He's letting people walking by know that he's got product to sell without overtly implicating himself. That pat of his coat pocket and the quick bend of his arm tells them it's heroin."

"Since the first day I found out TJ was using, I've been trying to answer this question: Why would anyone do that to themselves?"

"I'm married to a man who faces it every day. He's a physician at a clinic that specializes in drug use and overall quality of life for patients. I feel so guilty some days for dragging him up here. He's just a country bumpkin who loved living in sleepy little Edenville, North Carolina, delivering babies and eating at the local diner. But I needed to be up here; I needed to be doing things like this for my own sanity, and he's made it work." Willow took a sip of her coffee, never letting her eyes drift from Dante.

"That's incredible dedication to each other," Tara said, burying the envy she felt beneath a smile. "So does Josh know the answer to that question? Why would they do it to themselves?"

"My husband is a clinical man. He'd tell you the list of things that heroin does to a body, how the addiction is incessant and biological. But I know that's not what you're asking. My answer to that question is always different than his. Why does the person put that first needle in their arm? What did they need; what were they desperate for? Release? Escape? The rest of us are stuck facing all the horribly unfair, seemingly insurmountable piles of bullshit the world throws our way. There is no way around it, only through it. So we grab on to the people we love and plow forward. But remember the guy in the alley trying to sell to us, remember his pitch. Three seconds to rush. That's just how close the escape is. The shelter from all of it. Just three seconds away. It's street slang, but if you were desperate to be someone else, to feel like someone else, and you knew it was that close, maybe you'd grab it. Now the drug is cheap and accessible in a way we've never seen before. It's reaching more people and that proposition of a way out just three seconds away is too much for some to turn down."

"I guess for some people it's tempting," Tara sighed, still not willing to admit the tradeoffs could be worth it. "What's he doing now?" she asked, shooting off the wall to see better.

"Could you be a little less obvious?" Willow begged, tugging on Tara's sleeve. "We're supposed to be observing, not tackling the guy if he makes a sudden movement. Look, he's got a customer."

"We should do something," Tara said, feeling her heart thudding against her chest. "We can't let him sell drugs to someone right in front of us and not do anything."

"Of course we can," Willow said, sounding thoroughly annoyed. "The point of this is to try to see who he's associated with and why he was at the scene the night you were found."

"I'm still not sure why you think he was," Tara admitted, forcing herself to lean against the wall again and sip on her now lukewarm coffee.

"He's not that bright. He made the 911 call on a burner phone. That's great for anonymity if you ditch the phone. Figuratively burn it. But this idiot is still using the thing. You're supposed to buy it with cash too, which you'd think a drug dealer would have plenty of, but he used his prepaid debit card and bought it at a store that had some pretty high-tech cameras. Once my friend did a trap and trace on the number that made the emergency call, it was pretty easy connecting the dots."

"How did you get the number in the first place?" Tara asked, whispering as some random girls in far too little clothes sauntered by.

"I work off the barter system," Willow admitted with a smirk. "Everything in this business is about favors and keeping them in balance. You don't want to owe too many, and you don't want to call too many in all at once. It's a currency. I called in a few favors on this one, but I'm hoping they pay off. If the timeline from the dealer we saw in the alley is right, the police were already on their way when he saw you. Considering how much heroin was in your system you would have been administered the Narcan very quickly. This guy, or his phone anyway, made the 911 call, which means he may know what happened. He could be actively involved."

"But what will watching him tell us?" Tara asked, pulling her hat a little lower, feeling like too many eyes were on her.

"When you do work like this you don't always get concrete answers. Some things are a bust. Some are jackpots. It's a gamble."

"That's why you do it? It's exciting sometimes?" Tara asked, taking her focus off the stranger and watching Willow's profile. She was an intriguing woman, an ebb and flow of strength and insight.

"I do this because if I don't I can't sleep," she admitted between sips of coffee and zipping her coat up to her chin. "Everyone has a cross to carry, Tara. Mine is old; it's heavy and covered with names of people whose faces I will never forget. I can't help them, but I can help others. I have to."

"What if this is a dead end?" Tara asked, glancing back at the stranger who twitched and hopped anxiously as he talked to people passing by.

"Then we can try something else," Willow assured her, but her attention was quickly pulled away from the other conversation. "He's getting a call," she said, suddenly moving off the wall and crossing the street. "I want to hear this. Stay here."

"But," Tara protested, wanting to help.

Willow's head spun toward her and shot the age old *not screwing around* mother stare that couldn't be ignored. "Stay," she ordered again. Tara bit down on her bottom lip as Willow jogged across the street and pretended to be waving at someone behind Dante. It was probably no more than two minutes but standing there alone felt like it stretched over an hour.

When Willow finally came back across the street, puffing out clouds of warm breath, she launched right into the details. "He's meeting someone at the hospital in an hour. We need to stay on him. Maybe that's where he got the needle, just like the guy in the alley said. It was bigger than what you normally see on the street. We need to stay with him."

Before Tara could answer, her phone rang and she juggled it awkwardly out of her pocket. "Hey Reid, we've got big news. An actual lead."

"You need to come to the office," Reid ordered, ignoring the jubilance in her voice. "Have Willow drop you there. I need to talk to you."

"We can't," Tara explained with a breathy laugh. "Didn't you hear me? Willow is a genius. She actually tracked down the guy who called for help that night, and he has a meeting with someone at the hospital in an hour. There might be a link to the needle."

"No," Reid asserted coldly. For a moment she didn't answer, assuming he was talking to someone else, since his reply didn't make any sense. "Come to the office."

"Is everything all right? Did you see Wylie this morning?" Tara asked, turning to Willow for some kind of direction. "He says we need to go back to his office right now," she mouthed.

"No," Willow said, gesturing for Tara to hand the phone over. "Listen Reid, this is something I need to chase down. It's a legitimate lead."

Tara's eyes danced across Willow's face, dying to know what Reid was saying now. Of course he wouldn't want them to give up on it now.

"I'll put her in a cab," Willow said solemnly, not looking over at Tara now. "She'll be there in thirty minutes. But Reid—" She pulled the phone from her ear and stared at the screen. The line had been disconnected. "You've got to go see Reid. I'll handle this."

"Why? What is this about?" Tara asked, a wash of nausea rolling over her body. The expression on Willow's face was hauntingly ominous.

"I'll handle this. You need to go talk to Reid. He's in a fit about something, and you need to work it out. I can't keep up with you two. One minute you're on the same page the next you're fighting again. Grab a cab, and I'll check in with you after."

Willow was already heading toward her car before Tara could beg for more details. Last night with Reid had been rejuvenating. His support had emboldened her to believe she could get through this. The thought of him in the same room as Wylie, making sure he was all right, was everything. Knowing he was pissed off about something had her throat seizing up. Apparently vowing to support her was a fickle promise.

Chapter Twenty-Five

Reid saw her get out of the cab and fumble some cash to the driver. He'd been staring out his office window since Willow hung up, even though he knew Tara was a minimum of thirty minutes out. He wanted to see her before she saw him, to get eyes on her and try to remember what was right and what was wrong. From far away, down below him where she looked small and unfamiliar, he could remind himself of everything the Oldens had told him. From up here he could hold tight to his judgment that this had gone on long enough.

When she walked into his office, winded and her hair static and unruly from the hat she'd just yanked off, he chanted to himself to remember. "You scared the hell out of me, Reid. Is everything all right with Wylie?"

"Right now?" he asked, so much condescension in his voice that he saw it wound her. "Yes, he seems fine. Happy really. But the Oldens were not pleased to see me."

"I'm sorry," she nodded, as if she knew what this was about now. "They have very strong personalities, and you can't convince them of anything. Trust me I've tried. I'm sorry you had to deal with them today, but I do appreciate you trying. I should have warned you."

Reid wouldn't sit. Sitting was too weak, too friendly, for this moment. Instead he folded his arms over his chest and stared at her as she sank into a chair. "I think you need to consider what's best for Wylie now."

"You say that as though I'd be starting something new. All I do is think about what's best for him. I'm what's best." She wrinkled her nose and scrutinized him. "What exactly are you saying?"

"The Oldens have a solid case against you. With the best lawyer, I still think you'd be unlikely to retain your parental rights if you try to fight them."

"Are you telling me to give them Wylie? He's not an old sweater I don't wear anymore; he's my son. If they want to take him from me, you better believe I'm going to fight them. How solid could their case be? Your friend Kay said that as his biological parent there is precedence that the court will be in my favor."

"He burned himself on the stove? With that kid you call a babysitter? They know everything, Tara. They've dug about as deep as you can. You didn't even take him to the hospital?" The look on his face was rooted in betrayal. Tara had looked him dead in the eye and promised that Wylie was safe and happy with her. But now he had so many reasons to doubt that. He held some responsibility in taking what she said at face value.

"The woman upstairs treated the burn, and it was fine. It healed. Do you know what emergency rooms by us look like? It's not some cheery place with lots of friendly people. It's gunshot wounds and crackheads. Wylie was all right."

"The woman upstairs is a dental assistant, not a nurse, not a doctor. And trust me, that's not what they are building their case on. There was a stack, Tara." He gestured with his hands to show how high the papers mounted back at the Oldens'. Perhaps he exaggerated by an inch or two, but what did it really matter now? It all added up to the same thing.

"Of course they would," Tara scoffed, and it enraged him more. "Didn't you think they would twist everything? Haven't you been doing this job long enough to realize people will stop at nothing to get their way? Last night you said you were with me on this. That didn't last very long. The first time someone gives you a reason, you bail on me." She shot up from the chair and shook her head disappointedly at him.

"Tara, there has to be something there for them to twist. They aren't making this stuff up. Your pediatrician isn't going to go on record in a courtroom and lie. The pictures they have of your apartment don't lie."

"Why do they have pictures of my apartment?" she asked, gesturing wildly with her hands. "They can't do that."

"You shouldn't be worried about how they did it, you should be worried about how they intend to use what they have. You have roaches. Dirty laundry piled high. Complaints about the smell. Social services will be in there, you know that, right? They'll evaluate your house and these photos will be used in court." With a sudden sense of losing the battle but hoping to win the war, he settled his voice from a roar to a near whisper. "This is why I'm telling you it's time to think about what's best for Wylie. You have options. We're working on the federal charges; we're facing those head-on. But the custody hearing, I think we need to evaluate all your options. You need to have an open mind."

"No," she said flatly, her voice settled now too. "I will not bend to them. I will not let their perverted version of the truth dictate my life. They can't steal my child away."

"He deserves a good life," Reid said, giving not enough thought to the impact of his words. Like a spear to her heart, Tara stumbled back. Slapping a hand to her chest she stared at him precisely like someone who'd been mortally wounded.

"You're fired," Tara edged out through sporadic breaths.

"What?" he asked, the bitter taste of his angry words still on his tongue.

"You're fired," she repeated, more steadily now.

"Tara, you can't afford another lawyer. You need me." He was smirking, though he didn't mean to be. It was just a natural reaction to the absurd stance she was taking.

"Reid, I don't want you to represent me anymore. I don't want your help at all. This is done now." She pursed her lips and took a few steps toward the door.

"You know what your problem is?" Reid blurted out, knowing it would stop her. And just like it had when they were young, a challenge like that in his voice had her spinning around.

"Let's hear it," she challenged.

"Pride. Everything you do, or the things you won't do, is all your stupid pride getting in your way. You'd rather go down alone than actually let go of your pride enough to have a better life . . . and to give Wylie one."

"Fine," she said, tossing her hands up in mock defeat. "I'm too prideful for my own good. I'm delusional enough to believe I should raise my son who I love more than life. You've pegged me right."

"If you love him—" Reid, annoyed by her sarcasm, slammed a hand to his desk but she was bolting toward him before he could finish his sentence.

"Don't you dare, Reid. Don't you say another word, because I *am* full of pride, and I hold a grudge. If you finish that sentence, I'll never forgive you. Ever." She turned abruptly and headed out the door, slamming it behind her.

A framed picture of meaningless art bounced off its nail and hit the floor. The glass shattered in shards across the carpet.

"Fired?" he whispered to himself in disbelief. He'd never been fired from anything before in his life, let alone a job he wasn't getting paid to do. Tara would have to be out of her mind to walk away from his help now. She'd end up in prison, losing Wylie for good, all to prove he was wrong. That was either complete insanity or absolute conviction. Either way she lost.

Chapter Twenty-Six

Her apartment was garbage. Tara could see everything wrong with it. She could feel the cold wind blow right through the rattling windows every night. But what no one could see were the tickle fights and the soothing songs. When Wylie wet the bed, she never got angry, even if she was exhausted. Even if she'd just brought the sheet back from the long trek to the laundromat. It wasn't his fault. He was just a little boy.

With a frenzy of pulsing anger moving through her body, she began to clean. No, that was not a strong enough word for what she intended to do. She would purge.

Not that it would matter for long anyway. She'd already been informed by all of her employers that she was fired. The first one to let her go was the newspaper delivery. The morning following her arrest she didn't show up, and they had a strict no call/no show termination policy. One strike. The deli had been more forgiving, but with all she was trying to do to build her case and fix this unthinkable mess, it was impossible to make all her shifts. They at least sounded regretful when they let her go. The school where she taught piano lessons had been notified about her arrest. They were kind, but firm. She was not to return to school.

Money would run out before the next rent check was due. This place, the one she'd fought to pay for, attempted to keep clean, tried and failed to keep perfect, would not be hers for much longer. Reality, the relentless monster that kept beating her, couldn't be avoided. Even if she won the charges against her, even if she could win against the Oldens in the custody case, she'd have lost the life she'd built. And starting over seemed impossible.

The night she was found in the alley was the off-the-charts earthquake. It sparked the tsunami, and right now she was in that place where all the water was being pulled in, drawn to the sea. The eerie, endless empty shore it left was lonely, and she knew at some point the wall of a wave would come crashing down on her.

So she scrubbed, she poured bleach, and she stuffed garbage bags because it was the only thing that felt like a release right now. Her hands stung, her eyes watered, and still the apartment was shit.

She had no idea how long the person knocking on her door had been there. Tara had been grinding her teeth too loudly to hear the tiny rapping noise.

"Tara?" Willow's voice called softly. "Tara, are you in there?"

She wanted to yell no. Even though that wouldn't make much sense. The only thing she wanted more than solitude was to know if Willow had any new information. "Yeah," she finally answered, rinsing the chemicals off her hands and jogging toward the door.

"I'm sorry to come over like this," Willow apologized as she looked around the apartment like a mother who'd come home early, startling her teenager.

"Did you get anything at the hospital? Did he lead you to anything?"

"No," Willow said, her face falling with disappointment. "I tailed him, but he climbed in a bay door for delivery trucks and I lost him there."

"Oh," Tara said, letting her distress show. "I fired Reid today so since he's the one paying you there isn't much more you'll be able to do for me. I appreciate the help but I think this is it."

"I talked to Reid," Willow announced as she moved farther into the apartment and closed the door behind her, signaling she wasn't in a rush to leave. "I'm sorry you guys are arguing. This is a really stressful situation." She fidgeted with the leather bracelets on her wrist as she tried to get Tara to warm up to the idea of talking this out.

"I don't have anything to say about it," Tara shrugged, grabbing her cleaning supplies and aggressively wiping the crayon marks off the wobbly coffee table.

"Leave some paint on there," Willow joked but she was alone in her small chuckle. "I came over today to let you know that I'm not giving up yet. I hope you don't either."

"You must not have really talked to Reid, because if you had you'd be here trying to convince me my child is better off with the Oldens. They have money and can shower him with everything he'll ever want."

"How'd that work out for their son?" Willow asked so casually that Tara almost missed how profound of a question it was.

"Exactly," Tara agreed. "I know that they are Wylie's grandparents, but TJ wasn't always a drug addict, and when he had a clear head, he told me again and again they shouldn't be in Wylie's life. Now they are going to have him forever, and I'm sick over it." She slapped the rag onto the table and moved on, gathering up all the little throw rugs that covered the stains on the hardwood floor. She hugged them all in her arms and reluctantly listened as Willow continued.

"Reid has never really worked in family services of any kind. He doesn't have kids in his life. There are parts of this he can't understand. And I'm sure, like many custody cases, they are exaggerating or just plain inventing some things."

"Isn't it black and white? I let Wylie get burned on the stove when he was here with the sitter. I ignored his pediatrician who wanted to keep cramming antibiotics into him even though all they did was upset his stomach and not help his ear infections at all. I put off his surgery clearly because I don't care about him, not because I did my own research and felt like it might not be the solution for him. It smells like pee in here all the time. The stack of papers with all my neglect was this high," she said making a sarcastic gesture the way Reid had.

"My son fell off the bed when he was nine months old," Willow admitted as she grabbed the rag Tara had been using and started wiping down the baseboards. "Two and a half years later, my other son did the same thing. Around the same age. They were both fine, better than I was when it happened. I've made plenty of mistakes and sadly I've made some of them twice. My son wets the bed more nights than he doesn't and the smell of urine is always threatening to take over my house. I swear they all go to the bathroom with their eyes closed. They never hit the toilet."

"No one is trying to take your child from you," Tara snapped back, not feeling warmed by this attempt to commiserate.

170

"I guess I'm just trying to say it's not all black and white. Motherhood has so many opportunities for failure. I've had my share. I've had to apologize to my children so many times. Josh is a saint for putting up with me most days. But I love them, and they love me. There aren't many things I'm an expert in, but I can spot the difference between people who want to hurt children and people who just need help. You love Wylie."

"Why is it so easy for you to give me the benefit of the doubt and so hard for Reid?"

"He doesn't look at the same things I do. He's not a mother. I'll be honest, after hearing what he had to say I was worried about you. I decided I'd wait to see what you were doing when I got here. If all the theories and all the worries and charges against you were true, then this rock bottom would surely flush them out. You'd have a needle in your arm or maybe too many pills in your stomach as you gave up on the bathroom floor. But you were doing what I'd be doing. My house is never cleaner than when I'm hurt or mad. I once washed the floor so angrily that I snapped the mop right in half by accident. I think it's because when everything feels out of control we try to rein in all the little pieces of our lives that we can actually do something about. So I get this," she said, gesturing over at the throw rugs Tara was still hugging.

"Why can't he?" she asked, sniffling a little but then instantly righting herself. Tara refused to shed a tear about Reid's reaction. It was energy she couldn't afford to give away.

"Did I ever tell you how I met Reid?" Willow asked, grabbing the crayons off the floor and organizing them back into the box carefully.

"No," Tara remarked thoughtfully, realizing it hadn't come up. Reid didn't seem connected to anyone or anything, but he was close with Willow and Josh. Tara had assumed it had been some kind of work relationship that had morphed into friendship, although it looked like Josh and Willow did most of the heavy lifting there.

"I was in the courthouse in New York, waiting for a meeting with a lawyer about a conviction he felt needed a second look. It was a Monday, and the place was so overcrowded that the news actually took a few minutes to spread. There was a man with a gun in the large cathedral-ceilinged room with us. He strode to the front bench and told everyone to sit down. Slowly people obliged, taking spots on the floor, against walls, anywhere they could. The man said his name was Mike. Aside from the gun, he looked average. I remember thinking he must be a mailman or bank teller; that was the kind of look he had. After a bit of demanding, everyone shut up, and the room was finally silent. Mike broke into sobs, angry bubbling cries about how his wife and two daughters had been killed by a drunk driver, who'd been in that courtroom the day before. He had walked free because of a technicality uncovered by the defense attorney. Mike was furious. The system had failed him, and he was ready to die, to see others die, in order to even the score."

"That must have been terrifying," Tara gasped, shoving the rugs in a bag for the laundromat. "Did he hurt anyone?"

"People were crying and begging for their lives. I kept thinking about my kids and Josh and how they'd get on without me. I really thought we wouldn't make it out of there. But all of a sudden this man, who I presumed was a lawyer, judging by his suit and neatly styled hair, walked right up to Mike. The gun was pointed at his chest, right at his heart, but the man didn't flinch. I could see his face, and he was smiling. They exchanged some words but nothing I could make out. Until the lawyer asked Mike what his wife's and daughters' names were. Mike broke down again, not with anger this time but sadness. He uttered their names: Jennifer, Holly, and Chelsea. I'll never forget those names. And upon saying them, it was like Mike woke up, remembering that his family would not want him to hurt innocent people in their name. After a couple of requests from the lawyer, Mike handed the gun over and fell to the floor."

"That's incredible," Tara said, grabbing a stack of tattered baby books and putting them on the toy box. She watched Willow's face grow somber as though that sad commentary she'd told wasn't the real tragedy of it all.

"Everyone wanted to talk to the lawyer afterward, to thank him and hug him, but I could tell from across the room that wasn't what he wanted. So I left . . . ran, quite literally, home to my family and sobbed. A couple of days later I ran into the lawyer in the cafeteria, and we joked about how terrible the coffee was considering it was seven dollars. He introduced himself as Reid Holliston and told me he was there for only a week, working out details of a case he had in Boston. Considering I wouldn't likely be running into him again, I took the opportunity to thank him. I told him I was in the room that day and appreciated what he'd done. But, because I never really know how to deal with people, I also told him he was stupid. He could have been killed that day, and a look crossed his face that I will never forget." Willow was stark white now, clutching the box of crayons in her hands and staring off so she could better remember the details.

"What kind of look did Reid give you?"

"I bet a thousand people could have watched him and missed it. But I'm kind of an expert on damaged people. I've loved them, lived with them, and run away from all sorts of them. So when I told him he could have been killed, he looked at me with disappointment that he hadn't been, and I recognized it instantly. If fate hadn't stepped in, there was a good chance I'd have let him walk away. But his phone rang. I stood there with him and grabbed his coffee as his hand began to shake so much he couldn't hold it anymore. Apparently his business card had been found on a man who'd just jumped from the roof of the courthouse to his death."

"Mike?" Tara asked, her heart aching for all involved, but especially Reid.

"Yes. Reid had given him his card and said to call him if there was anything he could do. He was the one who'd kept the man out of jail, and he only had to spend a couple nights in the hospital being evaluated. Then he was dead, and Reid was frozen. I took his phone and hung it up when it was clear there was no more to say. I don't know what I was thinking, but I got him to my car and took him home the way you'd rescue a stray dog off the highway before it's hit and killed. Josh, who should have been surprised by the unexpected company, was surprisingly welcoming once I quietly explained the situation."

"What did Reid do at your house? I mean did he stay?"

"For a while he acted like he was all right. He ate dinner with us. He had a glass of wine and sat by the fire

174

Josh built while I put the kids to bed. By the time I came back downstairs Reid and Josh were talking like they'd known each other for a lifetime. That's how Josh is. I think that's why he helps so many addicts. He doesn't believe in the theory that you have to hit rock bottom before you get help. Everyone, in every phase of their life, is worthy of help and a listening ear according to my husband."

"And Reid talked about what? I feel like he's so closed off now. I can't imagine what he'd have to say. I wish I knew."

"That night he talked about his job as a defense attorney, and how it was crushing him. He'd walked up to Mike that day in the courtroom, gun to his chest, because it wasn't very long ago that he'd worked to get a reduced sentence for a woman who was drunk driving and killed an elderly couple in Boston. Reid admitted that a part of him thought if Mike had killed him it would complete some karma or something that he'd deserved."

"Why does Reid still do this job if he hates it so much? I knew from the first time I met with him at the courthouse that he was miserable."

"I can't answer that," Willow admitted, but she couldn't hold back her opinion. "Part of the problem is he is very good at his job. Effective. But I also think he was waiting to make the change until he could go out on a good note."

"Doesn't he win plenty of cases?"

"I think he wanted a truly innocent person to defend," Willow smirked. "In his career he's had people claim innocence or ignorance, and every time in one way or another he's been disappointed. Reid has worked to set some people free, and they immediately reoffend. I think he wanted to remember it all in a better light. He was waiting, holding out."

"I think today was that moment for him with me," Tara said, distracting herself with the task of stacking stuffed animals in the corner of the room. "For a minute I felt like he had faith in me, and then it was all snuffed out. I can see why that would have affected him so much."

"He slept at our house that night." Willow laughed. "We never offered, he never asked, we just gave him a pillow and some blankets for the couch and he stayed. When we got up the next day he was gone, and we thought that would probably be the last we saw him since he was headed to Boston. A couple weeks later he reached out to me, wanting to know more about what I do. How exactly I was helping to reopen old cases and investigate crimes where the investigations weren't thorough. We met for coffee, and before I knew it Reid was a part of our lives and we were a part of his. The distance is what saves him from feeling too committed to us. The five-hour drive between us means I'm not likely to pop in at his house unexpectedly too often, and he's not supposed to show up for the kids' school plays. We've figured out how to love him and how to appreciate the way he loves us back."

"How in the world did he get so complicated? He was just a kindhearted jock with a gorgeous head of hair when I knew him."

"I have a feeling that's not all he was, even back then. I don't know exactly why Reid is the way he is or when it all started. But I do know that since you showed up, I've seen parts of him, pieces of his heart, I've never seen before. I want Reid to be happy, and I feel like you are a part of that equation. Selfishly, I don't want you dropping out of his life right now. I don't want you to leave it the way it is. He thinks the same old thing that always happens has. The glimmer of hope that you might be worth all the effort he can muster, every inch of himself, was a gamble he hadn't taken in a while."

"I know I'm not perfect," Tara admitted, patting the enormous pile of laundry in the basket by her feet. "He wasn't wrong about everything today."

"You need help, Tara. You need a plan. But that doesn't mean someone else should get your child just because you're struggling. Reid can't see that yet, but I think he'll come around."

"He doesn't have time to come around," Tara said somberly, realizing how few days remained for them to pull all of this together.

"You're right," Willow agreed, making Tara feel even worse. "That's why you might need to come around first." She looked at Tara knowingly and smiled.

"I hear you," Tara agreed, finally for the first time today smiling herself.

"Now grab a few more rags and let's clean until we feel better," Willow instructed, taking another quick inventory of the apartment. "I've never met a juice stain I can't get rid of."

Tara tilted her head to the side and appraised Willow curiously. "You are a very interesting woman, Willow. How exactly did you become all these things? Strong, insightful, funny, and maternal. I don't think I've ever met someone with so many unique characteristics all embodied in one person. What's your secret?"

"I'm the product of many women who wouldn't stop giving me advice," Willow teased. "Even when I didn't want it, even when I fought them, they kept giving. I basically ran away to North Carolina and dropped out of college. On paper that should have been the biggest mistake of my life. In reality, it made me the woman I am today because the people who saved me down there were relentless. Bold, loud, unapologetic huggers who told me two things: I love you, and you're being stupid. I'd heard each of those things before. I just hadn't realized until I met them that those ideas could exist in tandem. You could be loved and screw up all at once. That allowed me to lay some bricks in my own foundation and keep building until I found myself."

"And now you have?" Tara asked, sort of enviously, wishing she knew what it was like to be exactly where she was meant to be, doing something she loved.

"Hell no," Willow laughed. "I'm still building. But I go to Edenville whenever I want and remind myself I'm loved and dumb."

"I'd like to live there," Tara said, closing her eyes and imagining a fresh start. "That'll never happen."

"You never know what tomorrow will bring. If you ever decide to go down south, I've got a restaurant you should check out. The Wise Owl. Best pie in the state and it comes with free unsolicited advice about everything in your life."

"If I get through today," Tara admitted, drawing in a deep breath, "maybe I'll think about tomorrow."

Chapter Twenty-Seven

The apartment wasn't clean. Not for a lack of effort on Tara and Willow's part. The bones of the place were too disgusting to make it shine. It would have taken paint and a remodel, no, probably dynamite to really help the place. But at least the result of two women doing angry cleaning had it smelling fresh with clean laundry. Willow had helped Tara lug everything back upstairs from the laundromat and put it away before she left to spend some time with her kids. Being alone in her apartment again only reminded Tara how much she hated the quiet.

If she had felt like the idea of help, of friendship, had been elusive and hard to define, today would have been the perfect example of how it could change her life for the better. On a bad day, a terribly disastrous day, a knock on the door had made a fraction of a difference. While it didn't fix everything it still meant a lot.

There was another tap, but this time it wasn't on the door. It came from the back of the apartment. Somewhere by her bedroom. It was light but incessant. A steady stream of taps that drew her to them. Were the rats back? No, rats didn't make that kind of noise. Theirs were scratchier and sporadic.

"Hello," she called nervously as she approached her half open bedroom door. It wasn't as though she expected someone to answer. Whatever was knocking on her wall

179

surely didn't speak, but somehow she hoped her words would scare it off.

Tara thought about grabbing the broom, to arm herself in some way, but it was too late. She was already pushing in the creaky bedroom door with the old metal doorknob. It didn't open fully, stopping well before it should as though something had fallen behind it. She pushed a little harder but it didn't give way.

She considered slamming it shut and leaving the problem, whatever it was, locked in her room for the night. Grasping the knob firmly to shut it in a hurry, her plan was suddenly interrupted. A large dirty hand reached around the door and grabbed hold of her hair. She shrieked, still picturing some kind of beast, some rogue animal mutated after years of living in the sewer.

Logic returned quickly as a potent smell reached her nose. The musk was strong and unfamiliar. Stale smoke and spilled liquor were poorly masked with cheap cologne. Knowing this wasn't a monster, but a man, she began to fight. More screams, scratches at the hand that soon became an arm and then a whole body. But her effort was futile.

Dante Yule.

He'd looked smaller at the park where they had watched him. As he pulled her into the room and threw her onto the bed, he seemed gigantic. "Stop," she yelled again as though the word meant something. Surely he wasn't just waiting to be told not to do this.

"Quiet," he hissed, pushing a finger over his stained, exposed teeth. "If you scream again, I'll have to quiet you." He made a slashing motion across his neck with the knife in his hand. It was one from her kitchen.

"What do you want?" she begged in a whisper, inching her way up to the headboard of her bed. "Money? Do you want money?"

"I have money," he laughed, maybe at the irony of how poor he looked for a man gloating about money. "You wouldn't think so, but I've got money. And I want to keep it."

"What do you want?"

"I knew TJ," he said, his face completely flat now, the maniacal smile wiped away by the memory. "You don't remember me because you never came around for the fun."

"Please, TJ is dead. I don't have any drugs. I don't have anything of his if that's what you're looking for." She folded her hands in a pleading way and forced herself not to cry. Tears wouldn't help, she could see he didn't care.

"He was my friend, you know," Dante said matter-of-factly as though commenting on an old colleague. "TJ came through for me every time. But I sold him out for a chunk of cash. A big chunk, but still, that's shitty, right?"

"No," Tara coughed out. "No it's not. I'm sure you had a reason to do it. TJ would understand."

"Ah," Dante started, crumpling his face up as though she were ridiculous. "No, trust me, this is screwed up shit. He would not have understood. It's seriously the worst. But some of us are put on this earth to be the worst. Know what I mean?" Dante moved closer to her, a small step and then a few very quick ones until he was standing at the edge of the bed staring at her.

"Everyone has some good in them," Tara pleaded. "You don't have to do bad things if you don't want to."

"That's how I felt," he said, wide-eyed as though they'd just had this profound moment of connection. "That's why I called the ambulance. You were so messed up. I was high too but, like, for a second I just saw you, and I felt stone sober. Like out of body shit."

"You were there?" she asked, trying to catch her breath. "You gave me the drugs? Why would you do that? Why don't I remember?"

"The same reason you won't remember this," he said, yanking a cloth from his pocket with his free hand. "Chloroform." He grinned as though he were some kind of genius who'd invented the potent chemical.

"Stop, please. I don't understand why you are doing this. You don't have to."

"The world is dirty," he said, looking angry again. "It has to be cleansed. It has to be rid of all the scum who inhabit it."

"I'm not scum," she pleaded as he inched closer with the rag. "I'm not."

"You are," he said simply. "You are scum. TJ was too."

He clutched the rag so tightly she saw his knuckles going white. She pushed herself as hard as she could against the wall and searched her mind for a way out. Dante was bigger. He was armed. And he was high, likely giving him a threshold for pain that she couldn't compete with.

"Wylie," she whispered wanting her last thoughts to be of him. She'd failed him.

"Don't," Dante demanded shaking his head violently. "Don't do that shit. You did that last time." He pointed the knife at her and jabbed it by her face. "Don't say anything."

"Wylie is my son," she edged out, wincing as the knife waved by her face again. "He won't remember me. He won't remember his dad." She was crying now, too afraid to keep the tears back. They might not help her survive but they were hers to cry if she wanted to.

"Don't," he demanded, slashing the knife closer this time and cutting her cheek. She felt her skin break open and watched the top of her white shirt soak with red. Instinctively her hand flew to the cut, knocking the knife from Dante, who looked stunned by the sight of blood. A queasy look washed over him as she pulled her hand down and more dripped off her chin. The second hesitation on his part was all she needed, lunging for the knife that had landed on the pillow. A second later he was on her, his hand clawing for the blade. But she'd already spun it around, and forced it through his hand.

Dante sprang backward off the bed and stumbled to his feet, screaming loudly, his eyes locked on the knife through his palm. Rolling off the opposite side of the bed, Tara made her way out of the room to arm herself with another knife or try to make it to the front door. His thudding footsteps made the decision for her. She'd never make it to the door and get the locks undone before he could reach her. The chloroform, she imagined, would only take a moment or two if he got back full control of the situation.

Dodging into the small kitchen she snatched a knife from the drawer and flung the oven door open. At least it would form some kind of space between them, and he'd have to maneuver to get around or over it. He was still screaming, louder than she had when he first showed himself. Tara's cheek was stinging, and her face was a mix of salty tears and bright red blood.

Feeling thoroughly underprepared, she hastily grabbed another knife from the drawer. Unsure how it would be to her advantage, she thought some form of surprise would help. She slid the second knife up the sleeve of her free arm and held the tip of the blade with her closed fist. If she opened her hand the knife would slide down. Dante rounded the corner and breathed deep, terrifying breaths through his flaring nostrils. The rag was in one hand, the knife lodged in his other palm.

"Bitch," he roared, and he closed the gap between them quickly, easily kicking the oven door closed with a crashing thud. She swiped at him with the knife in her left hand and he quickly caught her wrist bending it painfully backward. The chemical rag that would render her unconscious was crushed between his hand and her wrist. She cried out in pain as her arm felt like it might snap. Kicking wildly with her right leg, she forced him to grab hold of her knee before making contact with his groin. His hand with the knife through it was reacting on instinct as it crashed onto her leg and sent the knife popping out and flying to the ground.

Dante bellowed in pain, which only seemed to heighten his anger. His grip on her wrist and leg tightened to a threshold she couldn't bear. But both her moves had left him where she'd hoped, bent down slightly, both hands busy hurting her. Tara's right hand, still clenched shut holding the tip of the knife, was free and his neck exposed. With lightning speed, she opened her hand, the knife handle slid to her palm, and she clenched it tightly as she thrust it into the veiny part of his neck, stifling the yell of pain he was attempting. Blood spat up from his mouth and covered the half of her shirt that wasn't already stained.

"Tara!" a voice called from the other side of the door as Dante's full weight fell on her. Tara was pinned to the wall, her hand still on the knife that protruded from Dante's neck as she heard her front door being kicked in. "Tara," the voice called again.

It took her last bit of breath under Dante's dead weight to call back. "Reid. Kitchen."

Chapter Twenty-Eight

Reid wasn't bothered by blood. Or so he thought. His father had forced him through enough hunting trips. He'd seen his share of gruesome crime scene photos. But there was something wholly different about seeing someone you loved bloodied horror movie style as she lay across her kitchen floor.

There wasn't enough time to blink before the police were at his back, demanding he get on the ground and show them his hands. Someone must have called when they heard the same screaming he had. Their voices were muted by the ringing in his ears, but he still reacted as he thought he should. Of course they'd assume he was a suspect. Of course they'd need to control the situation.

Reid was tugged backward, pulled into the living room, and patted down. "Reid?" a familiar voice questioned as a crowd of people thundered into the room. "Dude, is that you? What happened?" Price Olivander was a detective Reid had worked with dozens of times. He was a go-to when Reid needed something he couldn't get through normal channels. Nothing illegal, just dancing on the line of unethical. He went by Olly to all who knew him, and Reid was relieved to see him.

Blinking hard and trying to balance himself, Reid focused in on the blue eyes of the familiar detective and tried to explain. He was grateful that Olly had shoved the other cops back and told them to lay off.

"You couldn't have caught this case already," Olly said in a half laugh. "The blood's still wet."

"She's my friend," he choked out, taking a few steps toward the kitchen when he realized Tara was still in there and needed help.

"Shit," Olly said, shaking his head apologetically. "Come on, you can't be in here. We need to clear the apartment."

"No," Reid insisted, shaking him off. "I need to be with her." The grip on his arms was so tight he knew he'd have to throw some punches if he was going to break free.

"EMTs are already in there. Let them do their thing. You'll only be in the way. Come downstairs. Tell me what you know," Olly pleaded desperately.

"I don't know shit," Reid argued, trying to shove Olly back. Other officers subdued him, and before he could argue his case they were shoving him down the stairs and into the cold air.

"Chill, bro," Olly insisted, a hand on each of Reid's shoulders. "They just called out an ID on the assailant. Dante Yule. He's a druggy. Looks like he broke in through the bedroom window and waited for her. Lots of information pouring in."

"No," Reid said, balling his fists in fury. "That son of a bitch. He must have followed her here."

"Did she know him?" Olly asked, turning quickly from a friendly questioning to an investigation. Reid was glad to hear it. He wanted answers too and Olly was the right man for the job. Relentless and quick, he'd seen Olly chase down plenty of leads.

"Tara was arrested for child endangerment for overdosing in an alley and leaving her kid alone in the cold," Reid started.

"I heard about that one," Olly said, squinting to jog his memory for the details. "They used Narcan on her; I know the officer who did it."

"I'm representing her. She has absolutely no history of habitual drug use, no evidence that she would abandon her child. I was running down a lead with an investigator, and we worked out that Dante was the one who called 911. Tara and the investigator tailed him today. I don't know, maybe he got spooked and tracked her here. Damn it." He punched his clenched fist into his palm. "I've got to get back up there."

"Hey," Olly said, flagging down another detective. They'd moved to the side of the apartment building, out of the way of emergency personnel and far enough from the ambulance sirens so they could hear each other.

"What's up, Olly?" the second detective asked, pushing his large glasses up his nose. He looked like a kid, the only thing validating he was a cop was the large badge dangling around his neck. Otherwise he might be confused for a Boy Scout.

"Liam, what do we know about this Yule guy? He's in the system obviously." Olly reached for his phone and started typing frantically.

"I already checked him out. This guy's Teflon. He's got to be a CI. They found a rag with chloroform on it. So this was planned."

"An informant?" Reid asked, wondering who would be dealing with this bastard, cutting deals for information.

"Is he in the database?" Olly asked, pacing around.

"Not that I can see," Liam replied, looking again. "But no one gets arrested this many times and walks. He's getting off with hardly anything every time. And has been doing it for years."

"Not possible," Olly argued, dismissing the kid's credibility. "If he'd been ratting that long he'd have been killed in the street by now. And there's no record of him as an informant anywhere or for anyone on the force. Something else has to be up. Stay on it, Liam, and let me know what you find." Olly gestured with his chin for the young detective to head out.

"This bastard better be dead or I'm going kill him. And she, she better be—" Reid felt like he might be sick if he didn't get answers soon.

"You can't help her right now, but you can help me. Tell me what else you know about this guy. Is there a chance she owed him some money? Was he her pimp?"

"She's clean," Reid shouted. "I told you that. She wasn't mixed up with this shit before they found her in that alley."

"All right," Olly said, putting his hands up apologetically. "I just want to get to the bottom of why he felt the need to attack her."

"Promise me something," Reid pleaded desperately. The look on Ollys's face spoke volumes. Reid was an even-keeled man who kept his temper in check. Every interaction these two had was always rooted in professionalism. But now Reid was unapologetically begging.

"I'll do what I can," Olly said, thoroughly uncomfortable by the show of emotion.

"If you hear anything about this guy call me right away. I think he's the one who drugged her the first time,

189

and he came back to finish the job. But I have no idea why. I need the answer."

"You can't quote me on anything. Nothing on the record, but I'll make sure you stay in the loop. Just don't screw me over." Olly jabbed one of his fingers into Reid's chest and gave him a fiery threatening look. "This is off the books. But I want the same courtesy. If you find something, you give me a heads-up."

"Got it," Reid said, nodding his promise emphatically.

"If she pulls through, I can have a detail put on her. Make sure she's covered at the hospital. If what you say is true, and this is the second attempt on her life, odds are someone is determined. If it's just this Yule guy, maybe she's fine, but if it goes deeper she may not be out of the woods."

Reid nodded, not wanting to address the idea that she may not need the protection. What if she didn't make it to the hospital? What if Yule had been successful? "I've got to be with her," he argued again.

"Both ambulances left already," Olly said, leaning back so he could see around the side of the building again. "You need a ride to the hospital?"

Reid stepped to the back of the apartment and saw Josh calmly negotiating with a uniformed officer who was persistently trying to turn him away.

"I'm good," Reid said over his shoulder. "I have a friend here."

Chapter Twenty-Nine

"What's going on?" Josh asked in a panic. His brows furrowed together as Reid yanked him back toward his car.

"Tara was attacked." Reid spun, trying to figure out how long he'd been here, how long it had been since Tara had been hurt. "What are you doing here?"

"I told Willow I'd come by and check on Tara to see how she was doing and make sure her heart wasn't giving her anymore trouble. Willow had just left a little while earlier. She was taking the kids to the movies so I figured I'd come now. Then I saw all the cops and the ambulance, but no one would tell me what happened. Is Tara injured?"

"She was on the floor under the guy, covered in blood and not conscious. I got pulled out of there by the cops and I didn't get an update before the ambulance left. We need to get to the hospital now. Have Willow meet us there."

"But she has the kids," Josh argued as Reid practically pushed him into the driver's seat.

"I know a girl who works the daycare for the doctors' kids. She can watch the boys for a little bit. I need Willow there. If Tara wakes up—when she does—I need Willow to hear what she has to say. It was Yule who attacked her. They were tailing him today. I need to know everything, and so does Willow."

"I can go switch with her if it's easier. I'll just take the kids," Josh said, backing out of the area flooded with cops.

"No," Reid said quieter now. "I need you too. The doctor stuff, whatever they have to say, I want you there. You," Reid stuttered, "you're good with this stuff. I'm just not."

"Okay." Josh understood, nodding. "I've got you, man."

It didn't take long to convince Willow to come. The moment she heard it was Yule she sounded crushed by the idea that this could be her fault. She ran through the gamut of reasons why she was sure she hadn't been spotted. She knew no one had followed her back to Tara's.

When they pulled up to the hospital, Reid ran in first. Calling over his shoulder he instructed them, "Go to the pediatric wing and ask for Susan McMillian. She's waiting for you. The boys can play there. Then meet me wherever the hell Tara is."

"Go with him," Willow instructed Josh. "He needs you. I'll be right there."

Josh quickly caught up and met Reid at the nurses' station in the emergency room. "I'm looking for Tara Shiloh. She was brought in by ambulance; where is she?"

The tall thin nurse glared at him, unimpressed by his urgency. "Are you family?"

When Reid curled his hand into a fist and ground his teeth together, Josh jumped in. "I'm a doctor. I have pertinent medical information regarding Miss Shiloh's heart condition, and I'd like to pass that on to the doctors treating her. I don't believe they'll be able to find it in her medical records."

She looked him over, still unimpressed but mildly concerned. "We have specific instructions not to let anyone in to see her. There are officers at her door."

"I'm sure I know them," Reid insisted. "Tell us where she is and I'll deal with the cops there."

"Yeah that's helping," Josh said, edging Reid back toward the chairs. "Sit. Shut up." There were very few people in Reid's life who could successfully order him around like that. Luckily for Josh he was one of them.

After a bit of negotiation that Reid couldn't make out, Josh disappeared with the nurse. Left there sitting, doing nothing and feeling useless, was crushing. Just as he was about to shoot to his feet to go another round with an unhelpful nurse, Willow came bounding down a hallway.

"Is Josh with her?"

"I think so," Reid said, looking helplessly at the double doors leading back to the emergency room that could only be opened by someone with a hospital badge. "I'm going to lose it, Willow. I'm going to kick in that damn door in a second if I don't—"

"Reid," Josh called, swinging the doors open. "Willow, come on back. You can see her."

Reid took a deep breath, knowing at least she was alive, able to be seen.

Josh started doling out information in rapid succession, and Reid only picked up the pieces that mattered. "She was slashed in the face, and her wrist has multiple fractures. Due to the stress on her heart she had major palpitations and passed out. They're stabilizing her now. Putting a cast on the wrist, stitching the laceration on her face. But she's okay. She's going to be all right."

Not realizing he'd been holding his breath, Reid finally gasped out the air trapped in his lungs. "All right," he said, repeating the words. "She's okay."

"She's exhausted, but I told the doctors you needed to see her, that it was crucial for her safety that she tell us what happened. Detective Olly, I think his name was, is here too."

"Tara," Reid called in a childlike voice as he barreled through the curtain toward her hospital bed. "I'm so sorry." He leaned down and kissed the top of her head. "I'm so sorry."

"You need to back up, sir," a doctor demanded, forcefully pulling Reid back. "Those stiches are fresh; we still need to cover them." A long line pulled together by black knotted thread ran from just under Tara's eye down to her chin.

"I'm fine," she lied, wincing as someone began wrapping her arm tightly with some sort of bandage. "It was Yule," she said, seeming to remember the importance of the information. "He was the one who drugged me that night, and he was going to kill me."

"Why?" Olly asked as though the answer could be that easy.

"He said I was scum and he had to rid the world of it. It was like he was crazy. He said he knew TJ," Tara said, wincing again in pain.

"Who's TJ?" Olly asked, sounding annoyed to be late to the game on this one.

"He's my son's father. He died of a drug overdose eighteen months ago. Heroin. This guy Yule was on it, too, I think. He was crazy." Her lip quivered at the memory, and she couldn't right herself before the tears came back. "He was just throwing me around."

"Sounds like some kind of drug-fueled psychosis or something. If he has it in his head that he's a vigilante, cleansing the world, he's probably lost it." Olly grabbed his ringing phone from his pocket. "I'll be back in a bit," he explained as he dashed through the curtain and started jabbering into his phone agitatedly.

"No way he's just some nut job," Willow dissented in a low voice. "It has to be bigger than this. Something with TJ, some kind of vendetta or something. Did TJ owe anyone money?"

A spooky look washed over Tara's face. "Money," she said, using her uninjured hand to wipe her eyes, gingerly avoiding the stitches. "He said he didn't need money. That he wasn't there for money, he had plenty. I figured as a drug dealer he must."

"No," Willow said firmly. "Dealers with a business mentality have money. Users like Yule, who also happen to sell, are broke. They use up half the product themselves. They can never turn a profit."

Tara nodded. "He said something about screwing over TJ for a lot of money. Like he did something to backstab TJ, and that got him a lot of money or something."

"Good," the doctor said as he shined a tiny flashlight into Tara's eyes. "Follow the light." He turned toward them and the smile on his face slid away. "One more minute in here then you need to go."

"What else do you remember?" Reid asked, afraid of the answer. Not ready to hear her articulate the fear and terror she must have been enduring.

"Nothing," she admitted. "I just fought. I couldn't make it to the door, so I went to the kitchen. He was going to kill me. He had this rag, and he said that's how he did it the first time."

"Chloroform," Reid nodded. "He must have grabbed you in the parking lot of the grocery store and drove you to the alley."

"That's why there was no record of you on any surveillance cameras." Willow drew in a breath. "Reid, I need to talk to you outside." She tugged his arm.

"I just want to see if she remembers anything else," Reid snapped.

"Now," Willow insisted, tugging him again. "Before you say anything else."

"What?" Reid barked as they made their way to a quiet corner of the hospital.

"How far ahead of the police did you arrive?" Willow asked in a whisper. "One minute? Two? Were they out front when you got there?"

"No," Reid answered, annoyed. "I was there maybe two minutes before them. I heard the screams and I kicked in the door. I looked around and called Tara's name. There was some more commotion and then I heard her call me to the kitchen."

"Have you given a formal statement yet?" Willow asked, the importance of this written all over her face.

"No."

"And she hasn't, right? Just what we heard in front of the detective?"

"Yes, as far as I know. Why? I told Olly that Tara had been drugged and I thought Yule was responsible. What are you getting at?"

"Even with him attacking her, it's still her word against Yule's. She says he admitted to drugging her. But what evidence do you have right now that you didn't have before this? She stabbed him. This could easily be spun into a dispute about drugs. It's still her saying it."

"But he was waiting in her apartment with chloroform," Reid argued angrily. "You know she's telling the truth, why are you saying this?"

"Because you know damn well someone else will pitch it too at some point. There is only one way around it. You have to say when you got there you heard Yule admit to drugging her."

"What?" Reid asked through a breathy laugh. "Your whole philosophy is built on finding justice and the truth and you want me to lie, presumably under oath when it comes to it?"

"That's not my philosophy, it's my damn business slogan. It's what makes what I do possible because people need to believe it. But you know better. My life is built on family and loyalty to it. That girl is the closest thing to family you have, and she needs you right now. Sometimes that gets messy. Loving people, taking care of them in a real way, it's not easy. You want to run; I know that about you. But you need to do this." She was thumping her small finger into his chest and glaring at him.

"Yeah," he said, nodding. "You're right. It's the only way. I need to say I heard him say it. Otherwise there's a chance no one will believe her. We'd be right back where we started. I'll tell Olly I want to make a formal statement about what I heard Yule say before she stabbed him. I told him I didn't know shit, but he'll let me say I was in shock."

197

"Good. Get your story straight with her first and make it quick. Don't let the doctors or nurses hear you. I'll distract the detective."

"Willow," Reid said, catching her arm before she could jog off, "I'm not going to run."

"I know," she smiled, "because I will literally handcuff you to a chair before I let that happen. I will super glue your ass to your desk. I will—"

"I get it." He laughed, letting her go. "Love's messy."

Chapter Thirty

The room was quiet now. Everything had been done the way Willow had instructed and now the only thing left to do was wait and rest. Tara had been sleeping for about an hour, but Reid didn't have any intention of moving. He'd be one with the hard wooden chair by her bed for as long as he needed to. For as long as she needed him.

"Why were you there?" her voice asked through the darkness. He didn't realize she was awake, and he jumped at the sound of it.

"I'm just sitting with you," he said, quietly clearing his throat.

"No, at my apartment. Why were you there?" She was easing herself to a sitting position but stopped when something seemed to hurt her.

"Be still," he begged, his hand falling to her shoulder. "You went through hell."

"You were coming over?" she asked again.

"I was," he admitted, knowing her well enough to realize she wouldn't stop asking the question until he answered it. "I wanted to talk to you."

"To yell some more?" she asked, with a long blown out breath.

"I left my house with the intention of apologizing, then on the way over, I thought of more things to yell at you about. Then on my way up the stairs I was back to the apologizing. Then I heard you scream."

"I'm not sure I believe you," Tara admitted, sniffling in the dark. "I mean you weren't completely wrong. I could have reacted better and—"

"Tara please," he pushed back her hair and let the pleading in his voice come through. "Don't let me off the hook. You shouldn't. Especially after all of this. You begged me to believe you, and if I had maybe this wouldn't have happened."

"There was no way to know it was Yule, or that he'd come after me again. You went to bat for me and told the detective you heard Yule incriminate himself. I'm sorry you had to do that. I wish you wouldn't have compromised yourself like that."

"No," he said, brushing the idea off. "I won't lose a minute of sleep over that. You shouldn't have to be in this alone. You won't be anymore. I swear it." He crossed his heart in that simple way they used to when they were children.

"I believe you," she said, smiling until the change in her face must have pulled the stitches and her grin melted away. "I should have done a better job with Wylie. I should have asked for help. You weren't wrong about my pride getting in the way. I thought a lot about what you said, and I think maybe the Oldens do deserve a chance to be in Wylie's life. If they'll help me I would welcome that."

"You'll have me, too. And I know Willow and Josh will help in any way they can. Now that we've made formal statements to the police, I'll be able to get the federal charges against you dropped. I talked to Kay, and under the circumstances she agreed to represent you. I think she felt like you'd been through enough, and you deserved the best shot possible. If you go in with a reasonable agreement with the Oldens I'm sure, once they see what happened here, they'll be willing to come to some kind of agreement. Things are looking up, kid." His hand was still resting on the top of her head, occasionally sweeping the wispy strands of hair back.

"Is Yule going to live?" Tara asked, closing her eyes and looking like she might be reliving the moment she plunged a knife into his neck.

"Yes. He's out of surgery. They expect him to be fine. I am going down to his room soon to see if he's awake. I know he won't be able to speak, but I want to see him for myself." Reid knew it would take all his willpower not to smother the guy with a pillow. But there was some kind of closure he'd get from looking at the helpless guy strapped to the bed.

"I just don't understand why he'd want me dead," she blurted.

"I intend to find out. When he's well he'll go through psychiatric evaluations and the cops will grill him. He might have lost it, or maybe there was an old feud between him and TJ that he wanted to settle. There's a chance he saw you one day, knew who you were, and decided now was the time to get revenge. We'll figure it out. I know it'll be important to have answers, to get some peace."

"Where did Willow and Josh go? I feel terrible that they have had to run around and do so much for me. I'm sure they want to go home."

"They're at my house," Reid said, feeling timid. He'd taken a leap, and he wasn't sure he'd be landing softly once he told Tara the news. "They're moving you in to my place. Your apartment was a mess after the attack, and I figured you wouldn't want to go back there. My place is a little . . ." He searched for the word but couldn't come up with it, going instead with an awkward shrug. "But I figured you and Wylie could stay until you get back on your feet. You can both take the spare bedroom. It's kind of small, but it's better than nothing. Willow is kid-proofing my house as we speak. She keeps texting me, saying how much of a pathetic disaster my apartment is, but that she's improving it by the second." He rambled on, afraid to see her reaction to his presumptive behavior.

"Reid," she sighed. "If you'd have asked me, I would have begged you not to do that."

"It's not too late to move things back."

"No," she smiled, less expressively now to accommodate the stitches. "I just mean, I'm glad you didn't ask. Maybe for a while you don't have to give me a chance to say no."

"Everything is going to work out, Tara. You get some rest, and I'm going to get a few things straightened out. I won't be far."

His phone was vibrating in his pocket as he leaned down and kissed her forehead. Her freezing cold hand settled on the back of his neck and slid down to his cheek. He dropped himself lower and pushed his forehead to hers, looking straight into her eyes. "You're safe now. A long time ago I was too young to help you. Then I was too caught up in myself to be there for you. But all that's done. You're not alone anymore. Never again. I promise."

She tipped her head up and kissed his lips. For the first time since they were teens he felt the electricity he'd been without for all those years. He hadn't even known that was what had been missing from his life until it was back. It wasn't a passionate kiss, and it lasted only a beat. Maybe she'd meant it just as a thank you.

"I'll be back," he whispered as a promise, his lips still hovering over hers.

Chapter Thirty-One

"Hey Willow," Reid said, expecting to be bombarded with more complaints about how many liquor bottles she had to get rid of just to see the counter.

"Something's not right," Willow said, skipping the greetings. "I just can't figure out why Yule would come back after all this time. It's driving me crazy."

"I'm heading to Yule's room now. If he's conscious, I'm going to try to get more out of him. I'll pass on anything I find out so you can let it roll around in that magic brain of yours for a while and maybe make sense of it. Call you in a bit." He pulled the phone away to hang up but she was still talking.

"It's not like he has a bank account or anything," Willow said in that manic way she always did when she was trying to work something out. "I still have the information on the burner phone. I can see where some of the other calls were coming from. I don't know what else to do. I'm just—" her voice caught and suddenly Reid understood. "I didn't see it, Reid. I thought he might lead us to something, but I never thought he was a danger to her. I was with her all afternoon. He was probably lurking around and waiting. I should have spotted this."

"Willow," Reid asserted loudly, "you did everything you could. And I'm glad you weren't here. I wouldn't want you both in the hospital or worse."

"Reid," she laughed. "I'd have killed him."

He thought about arguing how much bigger Yule was. How he was brandishing a knife and rag covered with chloroform, but then he remembered the time he saw Willow take a guy's knees out from under him with a baseball bat when they were trying to chase down a witness from an old case in bad area. The guy had not been expecting the small-framed woman to be capable of swinging a bat that hard.

"You're probably right." He sighed in agreement. "But she's going to be fine. And nothing is going to happen to her again. I won't let it."

"Me either," Willow whispered through some emotion then recovered quickly. "But keep me posted."

Just like the call had begun, it ended, no formalities, no goodbyes. And that was fine by Reid. Willow was an outstandingly loyal, brilliant woman and they didn't need all the fillers that came with superficial friendships.

There were two uniformed officers outside Yule's room as Reid approached. "Is he up?" he asked, cocking his chin toward the door.

"Yeah," the shorter, wider of the two officers replied casually. Reid recognized him from a case or two he'd handled, though his name was escaping him. "Olly is in there. He said if you came by to let you in." They both stepped a few inches away from the door and let him in. The room was bright, even though the sun had already set. Every light was on.

"Oh good," Olly said, taking a few steps back from Yule, whose forehead was beading with sweat. "You remember that prominent defense attorney who made a formal statement against you? Here he is now."

Yule was intubated, unable to speak but he shook his head vehemently.

"Oh now you have something to say? Feel free to use that pad I gave you," Olly said smugly.

Yule wrote feverishly and spun it around. *Liar. Wasn't even there.*

"He wasn't there when you admitted to drugging the girl?" Olly asked, looking only mildly concerned.

Yule scratched down another word. *Exactly.*

"God, you're stupid," Olly laughed. "I'll be honest; I don't give a shit if he was there or not. I know you did it, and you just admitted to it. So I'd really like you to drop this bullshit arrogant act you have going on."

Yule raised his middle finger up as high as he could, until the handcuff attached to the metal bed frame held him back.

"See, something must be making him this bold," Olly said, turning toward Reid.

Reid grunted and nodded his agreement.

"I think it's whoever has been helping him out all these years. That's what's making him be such a son of a bitch right now. But I've done my research." Olly paused, rubbing his stubbled chin thoughtfully.

Reid watched as Yule's lashes fluttered nervously.

"Whoever has been pulling the strings for your freedom over the years, I can assure you they aren't showing up this time." Olly had this snickering laugh as he spoke that Reid was sure he must have honed to perfection over the years.

Yule closed his eyes as though he didn't care about these threats at all. His confidence might have faltered for a moment, but if Olly wasn't naming names he wasn't worried.

"We've been to your apartment, Yule," Olly said, sternly now. "Not that walk-up on Wilmington Ave you say you stay in. I mean your real apartment. The one you stay in with that girl, Cherry."

Now there was something, Reid realized. Even the machines attached to Yule agreed. His heart rate increased significantly.

"And in that apartment," Olly continued, sounding excited to relay the information, "we found a bottle of chloroform. Along with stashes of drugs and some needles matching the one found on the victim in the alley that night." Olly's combover was bouncing up and down as he paced the room, his hand tucked respectfully behind his back as he moved.

Reid appreciated him not using Tara's name. This bastard didn't need to hear her sweet name ever again. He didn't deserve to.

"There were loads of other things too. But you already know that. So we've got good testimony and some solid evidence. This isn't some drug bust where whoever you normally run to can bail you out. Whoever they are, they aren't going to be able to help you now. I doubt they'll care."

He grunted and wrote again turning the page around. *You don't know shit.*

"I don't need to. You know who needs to know? The district attorney's office. Because they are the ones who are going to file the charges. Now, I am a curious man though. This slippery little game you've been playing the last couple of years, it's intriguing me. And I don't like not knowing. It keeps me up at night. So if you tell me how exactly you've been getting out of all this shit over the years I might be willing to talk to the DA on your behalf."

"Wait," Reid said, tossing a hand up. "This guy doesn't get a deal. He would have killed if he'd had the chance. Who knows who else he's killed with this bullshit about trying to cleanse the earth of scum."

The words were like a trigger to Yule, who tried to sit up a little straighter.

"That's what it is, right?" Reid asked, tuning into the reaction it had gotten. "You were cleaning up all the dirty things in this world, but how does that make sense when you're scum yourself? Who made you this great power equalizer in the world?"

Yule writhed and his eyes shot open wide. He wrote again, this time sloppy and sideways but Reid could still make it out. *The church.*

"Ha," Olly chuckled, "you don't strike me as some altar boy."

"Yeah," Reid agreed, pressing down the path that seemed to be eliciting the most reactions from Yule. "What church would bother having a man like you in it? Not a man, a monster."

Yule flipped them off again and banged his head back onto the pillow.

"I say he's delusional," Reid continued. "Call psych and have him checked out because he's some drug addled fool who's lost his mind. We're wasting our time."

Reid turned to go, gesturing with his chin for Olly to follow. He assumed by now Olly understood the long game he was trying to play.

"You're probably right," Olly agreed. "Just a nut job."

Yule made some more grunting noises and wrote frantically across the paper again. *I am the blood. I am the word. We are the anointed.*

Yule threw the notebook at Reid, who bent down and picked it up. Upon reading the words, he continued on his path out the door. There wouldn't be any other communication at this point.

"Think we might have bailed a little early," Olly admitted as he followed Reid down the hallway, stuffing his hands in his pockets.

"No," Reid said, holding the notepad. "He was done talking no matter what. Let's let him stew a little bit. Let him realize whoever he thinks is coming to help him isn't."

"How do we know they won't? Sometimes stuff like this gets pushed through channels, and I get a phone call to cut a guy like that loose." Olly looked nervous, checking his phone again and again.

"Even under these circumstances?" Reid challenged, rounding on Olly and shooting him a fierce look. "You can't really think this guy will walk free again."

"If he does," Olly said, splitting away from Reid to answer his ringing phone, "I'll give you the first crack at him in the parking lot."

"Deal," Reid said, pointing a finger at Olly as he headed back toward Tara's room. Shooting a quick text to Willow with the new information he saw a cart pass by. Food. He hadn't eaten since that morning and Tara probably hadn't either. He'd grab her a sandwich from the late night deli around the corner as an added apology. The way he always did when they were children. That was how to win Tara over, feed her. Make her smile. Remind her she's not alone.

Chapter Thirty-Two

Tara's dreams were filled with images of Wylie. His wobbly run as he teetered across the quiet backyard at Reid's secluded apartment. His popsicle-stained lips and his cold kisses once the summer finally returned. A smile broke across her face as she woke to the idea of a new life. Finally, not having to face it all by herself anymore. She wasn't sure how they'd navigate the custody battle but for the first time she had hope they could win.

"Smiling?" a man's voice asked too harshly for Tara to assume it was hospital staff checking in on her. "I don't know what you'd have to smile about."

Her eyes fluttered open and a familiar face hovered above her. Todd Olden looked down on her with such disdain she lost her breath for a moment. His face was twisted and demonic.

"What a waste you've been," he said, stepping back and lowering himself into the chair by her. "And now because of dumb luck you'll be free, and you'll get him back. Even though you don't deserve him. You ruined my son and now my grandson."

Tara was grateful for the space created between them, but her stomach flipped with anxiety. "Heroin ruined your son. And the ripple effect of it nearly ruined your grandson. But I promise you, Wylie will have a good life." She sat up, looking at him earnestly. "I regret keeping both of you away from him. I've given it a lot of thought, and maybe I was wrong."

His eyes came up from the spot on the floor where they were fixed, and he glared at her skeptically. "Why did you keep him from us?" he asked, so pained it broke her heart.

"TJ had very strong feelings about it. I was trying to honor what I thought he wanted. When I did try to let you in, you both came on so strong, and I felt like you were trying to take over. But this has been an eye-opening experience for me, and I don't want to live the way we have been living. We were isolated and struggling, and life doesn't have to be that way. I know that now."

"She's too far gone for that," Todd said apologetically, dropping his head down and shaking it angrily. "She won't let this work out for you."

"Millicent?" Tara asked, knowing she was the stronger willed of the couple. As she thought all this through, she knew Millicent would be reluctant. "We can all talk about it. We can sit down, and we don't have to go to court and make this a big ugly thing. We're all adults, and I really believe you care about Wylie."

"We'd do anything for Wylie," Todd stressed, standing again and moving toward the side of her bed. "We've already done so much for him. We can't stop now."

Chapter Thirty-Three

"I get it, Willow, you want more, but that's all I could get out of the guy for now," Reid said, his phone tucked between his shoulder and his ear as he balanced a bag of food and a couple sodas.

"It's the Oldens' church," Willow blurted. "The words he said, the anointed. That's part of their church. It's very specific. And the phone calls. At least half of them went to a line registered to the church. It's not tied to the actual building, but church funds pay the bill."

"Wait," Reid said, freezing in front of the elevator. Are you saying the Oldens are paying Yule? They wanted Tara killed? No way. I sat with these people. They are normal, caring people. They aren't murderers."

"There's a big difference between being able to murder someone and being able to write a check to make sure it gets done. You'd be surprised who is capable of that. I'm telling you. They are involved."

"Shit," Reid said, dropping the food and drinks to a splattering end on the floor. "Get cops over to their house now. Have them take custody of Wylie."

"I can't just make that call. You need to get someone on your end to do it," Willow replied frantically. "I don't have that kind of pull here."

"Right," Reid said, persistently pushing the button on the elevator and then opting to take the five flights of stairs instead. "I'll get Olly on it. You come down here, and bring all the information you've got."

"I'm already on my way," Willow promised as she disconnected.

Reid pushed his way through the metal door at the top of the stairs and tried to get his bearings as he searched for Olly. The two uniformed officers were still outside Yule's door.

"Hey," Reid called to them in such an alarming way that their hands flew to their belts and rested ready on their guns. "Where's Olly?" he asked, charging toward them. "I've got new information. I need him to call something in."

"He hasn't been back since he got the phone call," one man replied. "We can call it in, just tell us what you need."

"I don't know if my word is going to be enough. But it's legit. I can promise you that. A kid is in danger, and I know if I could explain it to Olly, he'd be on board."

"We got it," the taller man assured. "Olly told us you're one of the good ones. He doesn't say that about anyone. Whatever you need, we're on it."

Reid gave them the address for the Oldens and the instructions to take Wylie into custody. "I'm not sure how they'll react. If the allegations are true, then they are the ones behind the attempts on Tara's life. They may be desperate."

"We'll let the team know, and I'll get Olly on the phone too so he can weigh in. That's crazy shit," the shorter man replied rubbing a hand over his bearded chin thoughtfully.

"What's going on?" another officer asked, jogging over.

"Lou you're supposed to be guarding the girl. Get outta here," the taller officer said, shoving the baby-faced kid backward. He stumbled onto his heels and flailed a bit before grimacing.

"I heard something come over the radio and heard you guys hollering," he defended, but his face was reddening with embarrassment. "It's not like she's alone. Her father-in-law is in with her."

"What?" Reid yelled, a shock vibrating through his body.

"Yeah, he got there a few minutes ago. I checked his ID and stuff. He was clear." The stutter in his voice and the way sweat began to instantly gather on the kid's brow meant he knew he'd screwed up. Bad.

"Stay on this door." The taller man grabbed the kid by his shoulders and slammed him against the door. "Don't move. Let no one in."

"Yes sir," he said, shaking his head obediently.

They all moved like a thundering herd toward Tara's now unmanned hospital room door. Swinging it open they spilled in to find the room empty. Reid slid in farther, flinging the bathroom door open to find it empty as well. "Where the hell is she? They had her plugged in to all these machines."

"He pulled her IV," the officer said, gesturing down to the small pool of blood and the dripping needle and tape.

The tall officer stepped back into the hallway and began shouting. "Lock down the hospital!" Yelling into his radio he gave a hasty description of Todd and Tara as relayed by Reid.

"I've got to find her," Reid said, looking down the hallway left and right as an alarm and flashing lights began to overtake his senses.

"They won't get out of this building," the officer assured. "This hospital has a state-of-the-art security system because of the high volume neonatal unit. They had two cases a few years back of babies being taken. This is a code black. I've been here when they do the drills. It's top-notch. We'll sweep every room, every floor. Just stay put."

The officers disappeared down the hallway, giving more commands into their radios. Reid would not stay there, because that was about the only place Tara definitively wasn't. If Todd had taken her down the stairs there was a chance Reid would have bumped into them.

A nurse ran by, a radio in her hand. "I checked," she replied firmly. "The video shows they went into the stairwell four minutes ago but they haven't been picked up on any of the cameras on the lower floors. Have them check the cameras in case they went up. Maybe he snagged someone's access badge. That would get him into neonatal, psychiatric."

"What about the roof?" Reid asked, accidently pulling the woman backward more firmly than he meant to.

"What?" she asked, looking frightened.

"Could a badge have gotten him access to the roof?" He was barking at her, making the fear in her eyes grow, but he couldn't control the urgency.

"Who are you?"

"Answer me!" he demanded. "The roof?"

"He would have had to have a pass from either someone on the code black team or the building

215

maintenance staff in order to get up there. I suppose it's possible. But that wouldn't make sense."

"Why not?" Reid pleaded.

"Because there is no way down from the roof. It's not an effective exit strategy. You can't reach the street that way."

Reid's heart leaped into his throat. "You can," he corrected, "if you jump. Does your

pass give me access? Are you on the code black response team?"

"Yes," she said, and he watched her clutch nervously at the badge clipped to her shirt. "But you can't take it. Protocol is—"

"With all due respect, ma'am—" Reid started but didn't finish his sentence, instead he pulled the badge quickly off her and charged toward the stairwell. With adrenaline fueling his body he skipped three and four steps at a time until he reached the door leading to the roof. Swiping the card over the keypad it beeped and flashed green just as he shoved his shoulder into the metal door. He should have been thinking about the element of surprise, about being tactical but the idea of Tara up here, maybe literally hanging on for dear life overwhelmed his better judgment.

"Tara!" he shouted, running to the waist-high brick wall that separated him from a fast plummet toward the ground fourteen stories below.

"Reid," Tara shrieked, barely getting the word out before a hand clasped over her mouth. Todd had a grip around her waist and another over her face, sloppily trying to keep her quiet.

"Todd," Reid said sharply but then leveled his voice and threw his hands up to show he had nothing that could be considered a threat. "Just stay right there, and let's talk for a minute."

"No," Todd shouted back through tears. "No I can't. I have to do this."

"You don't," Reid replied. "I promise. I know it feels like you are out of options right now. But I assure you that isn't the case. We can go back downstairs. We can explain that this is a misunderstanding." The lies felt hollow and nasty on his tongue. But he knew this was always the first attempt. Take the consequence out of it. Make the situations seem like it is no big deal. But Todd didn't look convinced.

"You don't understand. My wife. I have to call her and tell her this is done. That's the only way this can happen. If not," he said, sniffling and tightening his grip on Tara. "If not she'll end it."

"End what?" Reid asked, taking a few small steps toward Todd and Tara.

"All of it," Todd said through a sob. "If I can't do this, then she and Wylie will be gone. She won't let anyone take him from her. If she can't have him, no one will."

With that Tara's body whipped around, the back of her head slamming into Todd's face, stunning him long enough for her to pull away. Reid made his move, diving toward them, pulling Tara forward. But Todd managed to keep hold of the cast on Tara's broken wrist, latching on with all his might like a scared child might clutch a teddy bear.

"You don't understand," Todd pleaded. "I have to."

"Please," Tara cried. "Please tell me where Wylie is. What is she going to do to him?"

"She just wants him to be safe," Todd cried, whimpering like a child, still refusing to let go of her casted arm. "We'll all be together here or in the Kingdom."

"No, no, no," Tara sobbed. "No, you need tell me where he is. He doesn't deserve this. Please, he's my baby. Please tell me where they are." Before Todd could answer, the beams of multiple flashlights cut through the darkness in their direction.

"Freeze!" A cacophony of voices and bodies struck them all at once and Todd was finally ripped away.

"Wait," Reid said, trying to break up the melee of flailing arms and barking demands. "He knows where the kid is. She has the kid, and she's going to hurt him if we don't find them fast. Let him talk."

"Please," Tara begged, clawing at the most aggressive officers slamming Todd to the ground. "Please he's the only one who can tell us where my baby is."

"Hey!" a booming voice called from behind them. "I will start tasering you bastards if you don't back off." Olly was banging his flashlight against the large metal duct work to their left until everyone was practically standing at attention.

"Sir," he said, pulling Todd to his feet and dusting him off slightly. "I'm going to ask you one time, so I don't want you to answer until you've really thought about this, do you understand?"

Todd opened his mouth to protest but Olly threw him a look that had him obediently nodding.

"Good, good," Olly said calmly. "I want to know where that boy is. Uh-uh, don't answer yet," Olly instructed when Todd opened his mouth again. "I need you to know if you feed me some bullshit answer, I will

218

hang you over the side of this building. You're a crazy son of a bitch who has done crazy things tonight. And all these guys will cover for me." He looked around and every officer circled, nodding their heads in agreement.

"I don't care," Todd said, still crying uncontrollably. "I'll be with them in the Kingdom. If I don't call her in five minutes, then the best thing you can do is toss me over the side of this building."

"No, no don't answer yet. I wasn't done," Olly scolded. "I didn't say I would let go. If you don't cooperate I will make sure you live. I will personally make sure you never have the opportunity to join them. I will watch you myself, every second of every day if I have to. You won't be with them."

"You can't do that," Todd protested. "You can't keep me from them in the Kingdom."

"It's up to you," Olly said, shrugging coolly. "Make the call. Tell your wife you did what you said you would do, and you're going to meet her. That everything is going to be all right."

"It might already be too late," Todd said, falling to his knees.

"No!" Tara shrieked. "Please, Todd. I know you don't want this. I know you love Wylie, and you loved TJ. Don't do this because she's convinced you it's the only way. It's not the only way."

Todd reached into his pocket, sending a flurry of officers shouting, but they quieted as he showed them his cell phone. "I do love him. I loved TJ so much."

"I know you did," Tara said, dropping down to her knees by him. "I'm so sorry you lost your son. Please don't take mine from me."

219

"Clear this area," Olly ordered. "This man has a phone call to make."

Chapter Thirty-Four

"You'll know when I know," Olly said for the tenth time as he sat in his office chair and listened intently to the chatter coming over the wire via his earpiece.

Tara considered smacking him if he gave that answer one more time. How was anyone, any mother, supposed to bear waiting to know the fate of her child? "Reid, I can't take this," she said, falling into his arms and pressing her face into his shoulder.

"They're doing everything they can," he replied comfortingly, squeezing her tightly. "Willow's there. She's going to be with Wylie once they have him. She'll stay with him every second until he's back with you."

"We've got him," Olly shouted, jumping up and high-fiving two other officers in the room. "He's good," Olly relayed to Tara who was still tightly clutching Reid's arm. "They're checking him out, but he looks completely fine. If he gets a clean bill of health, they'll bring him right here."

"Here?" Tara asked, looking around the bustling police station loaded with strangers and wondering how she was supposed to reunite with her child here.

"You have a better spot in mind?" Reid asked, looking ready to go to bat for Tara if this became a problem with Olly.

"It's the middle of the night," Tara said, checking the time. "He's going to be so tired. I just want to be somewhere quiet with him. Somewhere I can rock him and hold him while he sleeps."

"It's too long of a ride back to my house," Reid said, thinking it over.

"Wait," Olly interrupted, putting one hand up to his ear to hear the information better. "They don't have Millicent Olden in custody. She was not with the child. There's no sign of her."

"She couldn't have gotten far," Reid challenged, clearly trying to remove the worry from Tara's heavy heart.

"It's not clear. The boy was found asleep in a crib at a property they recently purchased. It's about an hour's drive from here. There's an alarm system, and it was logged as being set over two hours ago. She could have gotten a good distance away in that time."

"What do we do? She's obviously unbalanced." Tara paced around, moving closer to Olly who was still distracted by more information coming in. "She'll never leave us alone."

"Apparently that's not our only problem," he said through a heavy sigh.

"Wylie," Tara gasped. "Is he all right?"

"The boy's fine," Olly assured. "He's already en route. But your friend Willow has dug up some more information on the church. And the detectives we have with Yule say he's corroborating the details. This is deep conspiracy stuff here. Multiple members of the church were involved in this. My first impression is it's more of a cult, smart enough to parade around as a church. Until we round everyone up I don't know if you and your son are safe. I'm going to get the Marshals involved, and discuss some kind of witness protection."

"No," Reid argued. "I can keep her safe. No one is going to get anywhere near them."

"Trust me, you don't want that on your conscience, brother. Let us help." Olly walked away, pulling out his phone and getting down to business.

"What does he mean, Reid? Wylie and I have to go?"

"Maybe for a little while," he said apologetically. "Just until they know it's safe to come back."

"I can't," she said, digging her nails into his bicep. "We've been on our own for so long, we can't just go back into that isolation. Or a worse version of it where we are stuck somewhere we've never been. I was counting on having you."

"We'll figure it out," Reid promised. "Let's just get Wylie here first."

"Wylie," Tara said, here heart swelling with joy. "I'm never going to let him go again."

"He's a lucky boy."

"I know; there were so many things that could have happened," she said, closing her eyes and imagining in horror how different all of this could have turned out.

"No. That's not what I mean." Reid smirked. "He's a lucky boy to have a mom like you. Not for one second did you stop fighting for him. You were drugged, cut, kidnapped, and still you got him back. That's what I've always loved about you, Tara. You always knew how to fight, to stay above water."

"I'm ready for a break." She grimaced, finally looking like she was admitting defeat.

"I can't promise you a break," he said, running his thumb across her bandaged cheek down to her chin. "But I can promise you a partner."

He kissed her like there was no one else in the room. It was a gentle yet passionate overtaking of her lips that pushed, just for a moment, the chaotic scene away.

"I love you, Reid," she whispered as they pulled away. "I don't know what that means right now for us. I don't know what's about to happen, but you deserve to know you are loved."

"You do too," he said, kissing her again. "And I am going to be around to remind you. Maybe we've got a few more things to sort out, but me loving you won't change."

"How can you be sure?"

"Because it started when I was nine, and it's never changed. I just didn't get the chance to tell you."

Chapter Thirty-Five

The bell over the door of the small family restaurant jingled, and Tara felt some of her nerves melt away. It was warm and welcoming, and she instantly felt a bit of peace. Wylie had fallen asleep on the ride from the airport and was still drooling onto her shoulder as she shifted his weight. He was getting too heavy to carry around like this, but Tara didn't complain. Any time he was in her arms was a good thing.

"Hi there," a thin woman with brown and gray streaked hair said as she tossed a dishrag over her shoulder and tucked a pencil behind her ear. "Welcome to the Wise Owl. Can I get you a table?"

"I'm here to see Betty," she whispered, but then cleared her throat and tried again with a little more confidence. The cast was still on her arm. The stitches still in her cheek. "Sorry, I'm supposed to meet a woman named Betty."

"Well, that's me," Betty sang out, moving right toward them and patting Wylie gently on the back. "He's out cold, isn't he? Looks pretty heavy. Would you like to lay him down?"

"Here?" Tara asked, feeling both bad for intruding and unsure where Wylie could finish his nap.

"I've got an office right upstairs. There's a small apartment up there too. He could sleep while you and I talk. What's your name, dear?" Betty blinked her warm brown eyes that wrinkled more around the edges as her smile grew.

"Tara," she said, back to a whisper now. "I'm sorry if no one told you I was coming. I thought maybe Willow had arranged something. I don't want to be in the way."

"I don't think Willow wanted anyone to know you were coming. She sent me a quick message saying to be on the lookout for friends of hers."

"That was all?" Tara asked, having hoped there would be more in Edenville, North Carolina for her to depend on than just a woman who didn't know her name.

"That's all she needed to say. Any friend of Willow's is a friend of mine. You are welcome here. You are safe here," she added, lowering her rich velvety voice to a whisper. "Well, not safe from everything," she corrected, her face falling serious.

"No?" Tara asked, looking nervous.

"I can't protect you from the ten pounds you will gain from living upstairs from this restaurant. I cannot protect you from my grandchildren who will treat your son here like their own personal baby doll. My daughter and daughter-in-law cannot be controlled when it comes to butting in on your life and being completely overbearing in their attempt to make you feel welcome. I'm a strong woman, but you are on your own for those things."

"I can stay in the apartment upstairs?" Tara asked as they moved toward the back of the restaurant, savory smells filling her nose.

"Come on up, I'll show you around. You might not be too excited once you see it. It's small, gets a bit hot in the summertime. Always smells like chicken or pie, depending on the time of day."

"All of that sounds wonderful," Tara whispered, adjusting Wylie's weight to one arm so she could wipe some stray tears away with the other hand. "I'm so grateful for the help. I didn't realize Willow hadn't told you who I was or why I'm here. Just so you know, I'm not a criminal or anything. I won't cause you any trouble."

"Honey," Betty sang, pulling Wylie gently out of her arms and tucking him into the bed at the back of the upstairs apartment. When he was comfortably curled on the four poster bed, Betty pushed back his sweaty hair and smiled. "Willow wouldn't send anyone down here she didn't think we could handle."

"She had lovely things to say about you," Tara chimed in, now feeling out of place. "You helped her a lot over the years."

"That's how you build your army," Betty laughed, showing Tara to the small kitchen where she filled the tea kettle and pulled two mugs down from a cabinet.

"Army?" Tara asked, taking the chair Betty had gestured toward.

"Yes. You see I pride myself on helping anyone and everyone I can. I will give you what I have to give, and I will protect you. I will slap you upside your head when you are being a fool. It's my job, and I take it very seriously."

"She mentioned that, too," Tara chuckled, finally smiling.

"But I am one woman. The world is a big broken place, and I can't help everyone. Some days that reality is crushing. So I create other soldiers. Willow is one of them. She probably still thinks we are nothing alike, but she would be wrong there. Our tactics are different."

227

Danielle Stewart

"You don't have a switchblade?" Tara teased, a natural ease finally coming over her.

"I prefer a shotgun. Never have to use it really, but it's the kind of thing you only have to pull out once to make your point."

They both laughed as Betty poured the tea and offered her a scoop of sugar. She nodded her thanks and glanced over at Wylie who was snoring peacefully.

"I send these little soldiers out into the world and hope they are doing all they can too. Then every now and again I get a sign that they are. You and your boy are a good sign."

"Willow saved my life," Tara said, sipping on the ginger tea and taking in all the charm of the tiny apartment. "I'll never be able to thank her properly. Or you. You can't imagine how this will help us. I won't overstay my welcome."

"Everybody needs a little help from time to time. I've sure received plenty of it over the years."

"Is there something here I can do? I've waitressed before. Any job openings downstairs? I'd have to find a place for Wylie, some childcare, but once I do I'll be glad to do my share. I want to work."

"My daughter, Jules, would be glad to keep him during your shifts if you want afternoons and evenings. She's got a little boy, Ian, who's always looking for a playmate after school. Some days it's easier to have two little ones rather than just the one. It'll give her a break from playing Legos and cards all afternoon."

"I'd be so grateful," Tara beamed. "Why would you do this for me? All of you, why would you help me without really even knowing why I'm here or what I've done? You don't owe me anything. Willow and I met not that long ago. It's not like we're old friends."

"We do have an agenda," Betty admitted, hiding her smile behind her teacup. "We're always recruiting for our army."

"I'm not sure I'm what you're looking for," Tara said, hanging her head. "I'm not like you or Willow. I'm barely breathing at this point. Barely getting one foot in front of the other."

"I've found that's usually the best type of person to be," Betty assured Tara, patting her leg. "There's something humbling about having nothing, just surviving. I think it's because you never forget the feeling, and you recognize it in other people. Don't sell yourself short."

"Yes, ma'am," Tara gave in, though she wasn't feeling her plight was anything special yet. "I'll do my best."

"So, what type of girl are you?" Betty asked, the look on her face shifting to a light, playful expression.

"Excuse me?" Tara asked, unsure how to answer.

"Are you stubborn and moody like Willow was when I first met her? Do I have to hear your story in little pieces and weave it together on my own? Are you going to keep your secrets buried until they inevitably unearth themselves when you least expect it? Or are you just going to sit here and gab with me while gushing about all the things that brought you to Edenville? I like to know how much work I have ahead of me."

Tara laughed, closing her eyes and breathing in the sweet smell of her tea. "I'm an open book," Tara sighed. "I don't see the point in secrets. All they do is keep people away, and I need people right now. I can't do this alone anymore." She gestured with her broken arm over at Wylie. "I can't fight as hard anymore. It took me a while to see it. I didn't make it easy, but I know now, I need people."

"Hot damn," Betty hooted. "Then Willow really did some good work up there. You'll be one of the easy ones."

"Am I really one of many?" Tara asked doubtfully, pressing Betty with a serious look.

"You have no idea, child," Betty laughed, then quieted as Wylie stirred some. "Let's just say this apartment doesn't spend very much time empty. And we like it that way."

"Don't you ever get sick of helping people?" Tara asked, cocking her head to the side and analyzing Betty's face, which was covered with laugh lines that she'd obviously worked hard for.

"Sometimes I do," Betty said, sounding like she was admitting it to herself. "But I know how to fix it when it happens."

"How's that?" Tara asked, feeling like she was about to be given the answer to the meaning of life.

"Pie," Betty said simply. "Pie fixes everything."

Chapter Thirty-Six

"White, wheat, or rye?" Tara asked the familiar older couple who always left her a generous tip. As they finished their order she flashed them a smile and took the order to the kitchen.

"How are the Robinson's doing this evening?" Clay asked as he took the slip and began preparing their meal.

"Very well," Tara explained. "Their cat Mittsy is doing so much better. They are out tonight to celebrate." She let a little smile creep across her face.

"Not quite used to the small town pace yet, are you?" Clay shot her a knowing look. He and Betty were the perfect couple, running the restaurant and leading their large family through life. She couldn't believe that such people really existed. Their kindness and patience were boundless. Or so it seemed. She didn't intend to find out where it would end. Hopefully she wouldn't be imposing on them for too much longer. But news wasn't coming from Boston lately.

It had been completely quiet from Willow, Josh, and Reid for the last two months. That had given her plenty of time to settle in Edenville but also lots of time to worry. The lack of communication was calculated. Keeping Tara and Wylie tucked safely away in North Carolina while the depth of the conspiracy was unearthed meant she had to stay mostly in the dark. She had a sneaking suspicion

Betty and her son-in-law, Michael the lawyer, knew far more than they let on. But they deserved to be kept in the loop with all they were doing for her.

She and Wylie were now a part of Wednesday night dinners with Betty's family. Just as she'd warned, both she and Wylie had gained some weight, eating a litany of scrumptious foods as frequently as they liked. Life down here was good, and the support she'd always claimed she didn't need seemed to have come just in time. There was always a sitter for Wylie when she needed one. The women in Betty's family, Piper and Jules, were overbearingly welcoming in a perfect kind of way, and she found herself frequently commiserating and asking advice from the knowledgeable mothers. Bearing wine and old black and white movies, they'd show up as the restaurant closed and stay for a girls' night, turning the television from the upstairs office into their own personal movie theater.

But Tara missed Reid. She missed how they spent nights together before she left for Edenville. The way his skin felt against hers. The look in his eyes when he didn't have to crash on the floor anymore and he could hold her until the sun came up. But it was short-lived. Ripped away again by circumstance.

"Betty just called," Clay said as he rang the bell to indicate the plates were ready to be delivered to the Robinson's table. "After you drop these off have Sarah take over your tables and head over to the house."

"Is everything all right with Wylie?" Tara asked, always nervous when anything changed unexpectedly. "Is he sick?"

"I heard him laughing in the background. Everything sounded fine to me. She said she had something for you,

232

and you know how impatient she is. She'd never make it the last two hours of your shift." Clay waved her off and told her again that it was fine.

Piper's husband, Bobby, had found Tara a car she could use while she was there. It was nothing fancy, a four-door little red thing with a very high-tech car seat for Wylie. Bobby installed it himself, and every time she clipped Wylie in, she wanted to thank him again. She practically did, until he begged her to stop.

Driving down the dark roads toward Betty's house was becoming a habit now. Wylie was there more often than not, and the way he'd been folded into the family was enough to bring tears to Tara's eyes. It had escaped Tara before that her own lack of friends had made Wylie a byproduct of that. He didn't have anyone to play with either. No one but her to run to when he was hurt or afraid. All of a sudden there were a dozen people treating him like he was a part of something wonderful.

None of the usual cars were in the driveway when she pulled in, and her heart began to race in that fluttery way that sometimes meant she might pass out. She'd seen a cardiologist twice since she'd been in Edenville and her prognosis was good, but worry always seemed to take its toll.

No one was on the porch, which was strange, considering how much traffic the wooden planks got every day. Kids were usually sitting outside doing homework or the adults were stoking a fire. The light was on over the screen door and the kitchen windows were glowing warmly. But she didn't see anyone.

Tentatively making her way toward the door, she listened. There were voices and laughter, Wylie's excited cheers for more pie. It was still so surreal to Tara that she'd been plucked from the abyss and placed on this porch.

"Hello?" she asked, almost knocking before remembering how much Betty scolded her last time for not just letting herself in.

"She's here!" Betty chirped, practically yanking Tara into the house and straight into a hug. "You've got company."

Allowing herself to be tugged toward the sitting room, Tara braced herself for the surprise. Wylie scampered out of the room first, his arms stretched high as he called up to her.

"Baby, I missed you today," she said, smothering him with kisses.

Before she could get another word out, she gasped. Sitting on the couch with enormous grins were Josh, Willow, and Reid. "What are you doing here?" she asked, breaking instantly into tears as they shot to their feet and demanded hugs. Josh pulled her and Wylie in first. Then Willow, who after their hug took Wylie into her arms so that Reid could, for a brief moment, have all of her. And he did, folding her tightly beneath his warm arms. He held her as she cried and asked more unintelligible questions.

"There is this lovely well out in the backyard," Betty said, handing over a lantern and shuffling them out. Jedda, Willow's brother, built a bench back there. Why don't you two go check it out?"

Throwing on his coat and pulling on a hat, Reid whisked Tara out the door, down the porch, and back behind the house, never letting her go the whole time.

"I haven't heard anything from you," she said, her voice still broken up by excitement. "I've been dying to know what's been going on."

"A lot," he said as they followed the path toward the well Betty had told them about. "So much has happened, and I'm sorry we had to keep you in the dark about it. It was like a piece of thread and every inch we pulled something else unraveled. We thought about telling you, calling you a hundred times, but at some point we realized some of it needed to be said in person." His face grew sad as he said it, and if not for the bench coming into the light of the lantern and giving them a purpose to keep moving, she thought he might stop right there and break down.

When they settled onto the bench, his arms around her, she knew the news she'd hear would not feel anything like the joy she just experienced with this reunion.

"Todd and Millicent were most certainly not alone in these crimes," he started. "It was a systemic issue based on the idea that the world needed to be cleansed of sinners. It was deep and complex. I still feel like we've only begun to untangle it all. But many people have been brought to justice now. The church was basically a front to force people into treatment facilities run like prisons. Totally off the books and unregulated. They essentially forced addicts into them and some didn't survive the harsh tactics. We've found four cases so far and the doctors involved will be prosecuted. The church also employed men like Yule and convinced them that some people were not worthy of the treatment or had refused the treatment and needed to be cleansed from the earth. He and others like him gave dirty drugs to people,

235

resulting in their deaths. We're up to at least ten of those cases, but we think we're only scratching the surface. Yule believed he was a tool of God. He said he only sold the drugs so he could recruit more people for treatment and to have access to people who needed to be cleansed from the earth. The whole damn thing was outrageous. Todd and Millicent were actually involved in the cult before TJ ever started using. But apparently they were focused in other factions of it. They targeted prostitutes who needed salvation. But it was fundamentally the same thing. They'd break them down and brainwash them and add more people to the cult. We've made some substantial headway."

"Enough to consider Wylie and me safe?" Tara asked, her eyes dancing to every corner of his face which held a pained expression.

"I believe so," Reid said, though he wasn't celebrating.

"Don't you want that?" Tara questioned, wondering if maybe Reid had appreciated this time apart, found some perspective once the danger had climaxed and realized they were not meant to be in each other's lives.

"All I want is for you to be safe, but in that process we found out some things. Millicent was apprehended. Todd made a decision to work with the district attorney's office and his statement against his wife and the church was sobering. The admissions . . ." He closed his eyes. "There's something I have to tell you."

"What else could there be, Reid? Honestly they tried to kill me and steal my son. What else could they tell you that would be worse than that?"

"TJ was apparently deemed by the head of the cult as someone who could not be saved," he said curtly but then tried again, this time with more clarity. "TJ didn't overdose."

"What?" she asked, the statement overloading her senses. The idea that TJ was a casualty of the insanity his parents hid behind was sickening.

"They had him killed because he had resisted their treatment facilities. Everything they did from that moment on was part of their plan to get Wylie. They became foster parents to other children, creating relationships with people in the system. They reached out to you, knowing you would likely push them away when they tactically became too overbearing. They strategically aligned themselves to be ready to take Wylie when they put their plan into action. They weren't trying to slander you into losing your child through the courts. They wanted you dead."

"Why would they do this to their own son and grandson?"

"The theology behind it doesn't make sense and isn't even worth giving a voice to. It was insanity. Collective insanity that, to me, rivals any cult in history. This will be enormous in scale and the publicity will be crushing all around. If you were to come back to Boston now, you'd never be given any peace."

"But," she sniffed, a growing anger in her stomach beginning to flame. They'd already taken so much from her and now the light at the end of this long dark tunnel just faded out. "I know that you and I haven't talked. I know that the circumstances were very stressful, and I can't thank you enough for all you've done."

"But?" he asked, looking nervous.

"I love it here. I mean I love it in a way I never imagined I could. It's comfortable and welcoming. I have help and friends and so does Wylie. There's a preschool here that he could start in the spring if I wanted. I've almost got enough saved up to get my own place."

"It would be all right if you didn't want to go back to Boston," Reid assured her. "Especially if this is going to be in the press for a while."

"Reid," she pleaded, looking up at him as though he'd missed the point. "I love you. I've loved you my entire life, and I would live in a shoe box next to a garbage can if it meant that was the only place we could be together. I've been sitting down here this whole time, hanging on to the idea that maybe you love me the same way. That we'd be together. I need to know now if that isn't the case. Because I can be happy down here. I can be happy again, but I need to know if I have to let you go."

He didn't answer, his mouth opened and closed a few times but words didn't come. She could stand the truth, even if it hurt, but she couldn't take the silence.

"It's all right, Reid," she said, pulling away and standing up. "You don't owe me anything. You've paid your debt to me tenfold. Any guilt that you had about our childhood and what happened to me, it's good now. I'll be fine. Hell, I'll be more than fine. But I was not going to keep my feelings for you to myself again." She moved toward the well and leaned down, staring into the deep darkness of it.

"I wanted to have this conversation with you, Tara," Reid said in that lawyer voice of his that pissed her off. "I just thought I'd be the one bringing it up. I had it all planned out in my head."

"Sorry," she laughed humorlessly. "I know how important a plan is to you. I think we should head back to the house. I want to visit with Josh and Willow."

"Don't go," Reid said, standing and rubbing at his tired eyes. "Let me get out what I was going to say."

"Fine," she shrugged as though her heart wasn't in pieces. "But I'm not here for a closing argument in a courtroom. Can't you just talk from your heart?"

"A tall order," he joked, but she didn't bite. Dropping his head down he stared at his shoes, kicking around some dirt. "All I thought was that I want to follow this case through. I want to bag every single person who had anything to do with hurting you or using their twisted ideology to hurt someone else who didn't deserve it. I quit my firm. I signed on with Willow." He waved his hands animatedly.

"And I can't be a part of that?" she asked, doing an awful job of hiding the wounded edge in her voice.

"It'll be a circus. It'll be reliving it over and over again. You said you and Wylie are happy here. Right?"

"If that's all you heard," Tara groaned, nearly giving up on him.

"No," he cut in, by her side now, turning her body so she couldn't look away. His eyes fixed on the last remnants of the scar on her cheek, and it made her grow instantly hot with embarrassment.

"It's hideous," she said, assuming she was voicing his inner thoughts.

"It's the reason I'm staying," he whispered running a finger along the indented skin.

"Staying where?"

"Here, or close by anyway. I almost lost you, and you almost lost Wylie. No matter how much time and energy I give to the case it won't change what happened to you. This scar won't suddenly go away just because I personally found justice for you. I can give them everything I have of myself but what does it change?"

"I don't know," she shrugged.

"So I'm coming down here. And I'm finding a job. Willow and her team are more than competent to handle the case, and I'm positive she'd just say I was in the way. I can't take away what happened to you, but we can start something better. We can have a life together that makes everything that came before feel irrelevant and far away. I'm staying here."

Her hand flew to her heart as it fluttered dangerously fast. "I'm going to faint," she explained as black spots danced in front of her eyes.

"I know it's a lot but—"

"No," she said, clutching his neck tightly. "No it's not a lot. It's just the right amount." After a minute of deep breaths and leaning on him she felt more composed.

"I don't understand how you figured all this out. You've always been scared of things like this. Did you just wake up one morning and realize this was what you wanted?" She hoped he'd forgive her skepticism.

"Are you asking me if maybe I haven't made my mind up? Are you wondering if I made the decisions so quickly that I could unmake them just as fast?"

"Yes," Tara admitted, wishing she had more blind trust. "That's exactly what I'm asking."

Reid laughed at how well he could decipher so little words from her. "I didn't come to this all at once or on a whim. There was a lot of talking about it."

"Talking about it?" she smirked. "That doesn't sound like you at all. How did Willow manage that?"

"She didn't," he admitted, looking away. "Betty did. A lot of phone calls from that woman. She is persistent but in the strangest nice way possible."

"She bullied you into it?" Tara asked, feeling equally nervous about this prospect. Forcing Reid into the arrangement wasn't much better.

"Not even a little bit. There were no tricks, no persuasion. Just talking, mostly me talking, until I figured out what it was I really wanted. What was actually important. I'm not going to change my mind, Tara."

"I want to believe you," she murmured, feeling terrible for not being more convinced.

"You want to believe me, but do you want to marry me?" he asked, sliding a gold ring into her palm. "Because I want to marry you." He dropped to one knee and she nearly went with him. If he hadn't been holding her waist, keeping her upright she'd have bent by now.

"Tara, you were my first friend. The only one to see me when other people saw nothing. You gave me the courage to put myself out there and unfortunately I leaped and forgot to look back. I'm sorry I left you behind. I'm sorry I didn't realize how much you'd given me. The rest of my life will be spent trying to give it all back to you. Because you deserve it. You deserve everything. Will you give me that chance? Will you marry me?" He kissed her hand and waited for her answer.

"Yes," she shrieked, jumping up and down wildly, knocking him backward into the dirt. "Oh I'm sorry," she said, laughing and bubbling over with joy as she tried to lift him up. Instead he pulled her down on top of him and held her tightly.

"I've got you," he said, not as threat, not to tease, but as a promise. "I've got you now."

The End

Books By Danielle Stewart

Piper Anderson Series
Book 1: Chasing Justice
Book 2: Cutting Ties
Book 3: Changing Fate
Book 4: Finding Freedom
Book 5: Settling Scores
Book 6: Battling Destiny
Book 7: Chris & Sydney Collection – Choosing
Christmas & Saving Love
Betty's Journal - Bonus Material (suggested to be
read after Book 4 to avoid spoilers)

Edenville Series – A Piper Anderson Spin Off
Book 1: Flowers in the Snow
Book 2: Kiss in the Wind
Book 3: Stars in a Bottle

Piper Anderson Legacy Mystery
Book 1: Three Seconds To Rush
Book 2: Just for a Heartbeat

The Clover Series
Hearts of Clover - Novella & Book 2: (Half My
Heart & Change My Heart)
Book 3: All My Heart
Book 4: Facing Home

Rough Waters Series
Book 1: The Goodbye Storm
Book 2: The Runaway Storm
Book 3: The Rising Storm

Midnight Magic Series
Amelia

The Barrington Billionaires Series
Book 1: Fierce Love
Book 2: Wild Eyes
Book 3: Crazy Nights

Author Information

One random newsletter subscriber will be chosen every month this year. The chosen subscriber will receive a $25 eGift Card! Sign up today by visiting www.authordaniellestewart.com

Author Contact:
Website: AuthorDanielleStewart.com
Email: AuthorDanielleStewart@Gmail.com
Facebook: Author Danielle Stewart
Twitter: @DStewartAuthor